ESPIONAGE
IN MINIATURE

ESPIONAGE
IN MINIATURE

EDWARD R. LIPINSKI

ARPress
45 Dan Road Suite 5
Canton MA 02021

Hotline: 1(888) 821-0229
Fax: 1(508) 545-7580

Ordering Information:

Quantity sales. Special discounts are available on quantity purchases by corporations, associations, and others. For details, contact the publisher at the address above.

Printed in the United States of America.

ISBN-13:   Softcover   979-8-89330-355-1
                eBook   979-8-89330-356-8
                HardBook   979-8-89330-357-5

Library of Congress Control Number: 2024900514

CONTENTS

CHAPTER 1

As a young boy in grammar school, Jake Barrada was a good student. He was smart and got good grades. Nevertheless, he was a source of frustration for his teachers because he lacked ambition. It seemed that he accepted his present situation, but he never gave much thought to the future or what he wanted to do with his life. He never expressed an interest in any career field and he didn't seem to have any goals. It was as if he didn't care about anything. At one time or another, his teachers tried to motivate him but young Jake remained indifferent to the need to set goals in life.

When he was in the sixth grade, his teacher, Mrs. Meehan, gave her students a writing assignment. She instructed them to write an essay telling what they wanted to be when they grew up. She thought that this would spark their imagination and that they would enjoy writing about what roles they would like to assume in the adult world. Indeed, the students attacked this assignment with more enthusiasm than they usually devoted to previous writing assignments. At the same time, she noticed that young Jake Barrada didn't exhibit the same zeal as his classmates and she wondered what the boy would make of the assignment.

After three hours, the bell rang announcing that the morning session was over and it was time for lunch. Mrs. Meehan collected the papers as the students evacuated the classroom to go to lunch. While she was alone in the classroom, Mrs. Meehan read the essays that the students wrote. Most were interesting—a couple were amusing—but in general, they were the typical expressions and dreams of normal sixth-grade students.

When she read Jake's essay she was dumbfounded. The boy wrote that he wanted to become a drunken sea captain. Mrs. Meehan didn't know what to make of this. *Surely, the boy wasn't serious.* When the students returned from lunch, she confronted young Jake and asked him if he was trying to be funny. Jake replied without smiling, without mirth, without a hint of mischief, that he was serious when he wrote about what he wanted to be. He wanted to become a drunken sea captain.

Mrs. Meehan was at a loss for words. She certainly didn't approve of Jake's choice of vocation and she told him so. She wanted to correct him and point out the error of his ways, but she wasn't sure how to do this. After all this was public school—not Sunday school—and it was not her job to teach morality. She couldn't give him a failing grade for the paper, because it was well-written, with good grammar, no spelling mistakes, and organized in logical sequence. She had to acknowledge that it was a good essay even though his choice of a career was not to her liking. She couldn't discipline him or sentence him to detention because the boy hadn't done anything wrong.

Nevertheless, her high-minded sense of propriety told her that she had to do something to set the boy on the straight-and-narrow path to becoming a responsible adult. *Drunken sea captain, indeed!* Mrs. Meehan decided that Jake's parents should be alerted to the boy's wayward ambition. She sent a letter to his parents. In the letter, she said that while Jake was a good student his lack of ambition and his misguided career choice left something to be desired. She suggested that Mr. and Mrs. Barrada have a serious discussion with their son.

Jake dutifully brought the letter home to his mother. She read the letter and sighed. This was not the first time that young Jake voiced one of his foolish career choices, but Mrs. Barrada always dismissed his wild and strange vocation preferences as the product of his spirited imagination. Nevertheless, she felt obligated to reply to Mrs. Meehan's letter.

She sat down and wrote a letter saying that she and her husband were aware of Jake's foible and they believed that it came about because Jake had been watching the wrong movies, was reading too many graphic novels, and interacting with questionable people on the internet. She added that she and her husband would pay greater attention to young Jake's activities and hopefully they could readjust his values. Moreover, they would try to find some way to fire up his ambition and channel it into conventional and respectable paths.

Maybe their efforts worked and then again, maybe not. No one really knew because after that, Jake never told anyone what he wanted to be when he grew up or if he had any goals that he wanted to pursue. And no one asked him.

His teachers and other adults were aware that Jake always did what he was told, he followed instructions, studied and did his homework. At the same time, they recognized that there were certain shortcomings in his attitude—nothing seemed to interest him. He lacked initiative, and he was completely devoid of ambition. None of the teachers or administrators in the school knew how to correct those shortcomings but they agreed that Jake was a good boy and they assumed he would eventually find a stable career field and he would, in the course of time, become a success at something—although no one could predict what that *something* might be.

Jake advanced through grammar school and entered high school. While he was in high school, Jake continued to be a competent student but he only worked up to his level of interest and never put in any extra effort. It was obvious that he lacked initiative and ambition. Jake's teachers believed that he was capable of achieving much more if only they could find some way to motivate him.

Jake's English teacher, Mr. Theodore Devon, was aware of the boy's indifferent attitude and he was confident that he could find a way to motivate him. After observing Jake in the classroom, he conceived an of an exercise in public speaking that he was sure would arouse and excite Jake's interest. He explained to the class that each student would stand up and speak extemporaneously about what they wanted to be in life—what occupation they would most like to have. Devon explained that this exercise would teach the students poise, elocution and the ability to think on their feet.

Devon secretly believed that when Jake Barrada heard his fellow students talk about their ambitions and lofty career goals, he would be inspired to take a greater interest in his future and give some serious thought to choosing a rewarding career field. Devon was convinced that all Jake needed was a little inspiration from his peers.

Devon sat in the back of the classroom so he could watch and listen as each student stood up and spoke to the class. Lenny Rothman was the first to stand. Lenny told the class that he wanted to become a pediatrician because he liked children and he believed that a career in medicine would help people. Geraldine Roden got up next and told the class that she wanted to become a psychiatrist because she wanted to study the complexities of human personality and use her skills and knowledge to help patients with emotional and psychological disorders. Theresa Frey followed. She explained that she wanted to be a writer and she hoped to win the Pulitzer Prize someday. Then Carol Hanson rose to speak. She explained that she wanted to study mathematics and computer science and eventually work for NASA. Finally, it was Jake's turn.

Devon was sure that students' descriptions of their lofty ambitions had a positive effect on Jake. He leaned forward in his chair in anticipation as Jake stood up at the front of the classroom and cleared his throat. There was a brief moment of silence, then Jake told his classmates that he wanted to be a shepherd. He explained that he thought that it would be nice working outdoors in a pastoral setting managing a herd of sheep. He added that it would be a calm and peaceful way to make a living and would not require arduous study to earn a college degree.

All the students chuckled at Jake's quaint choice of a career. Devon smiled and pointed out that being a shepherd did have some bucolic charm but it wasn't a very practical vocation. Devon added that there was no future in shepherding and employment opportunities—if any existed at all—would be few and far between. He suggested that Jake take a minute to reconsider his choice of career and come up with something more practical.

Jake remained standing in front of the class and looked down at the floor as he contemplated another career option. After a moment of quiet cogitation, Jake looked up at the class and declared that if he could not be a shepherd he would like to be a pimp. There was a brief minute of shocked silence then all the students burst out laughing. Everyone was amused—everyone except Devon.

Devon was irate. *Did Jake Barrada actually want to be a pimp or was he just being the class clown?* No matter! Mr. Devon felt that he had to restore order in the classroom and at the same time put the young man in his place. He rose from his chair and marched to the front of the classroom where he confronted young Jake Barrada.

Devon tried to intimidate Jake by his physical presence and by exhibiting a menacing glare, but his efforts were in vain. He was short, and Jake, being a head taller than Devon, towered over the diminutive English teacher. Jake looked down with an expressionless, placid gaze that diffused the intensity of Devon's glare. Moreover, Devon was frustrated because he could not come up with a strong argument to explain to Jake why he should not be a pimp. Completely at a loss for words, the bantam English teacher told Jake to sit down.

That was the end of any attempts on the part of the school faculty or administration to motivate young Jake or instill a sense of proper moral values. They did tell him, however, that he should plan to go to college and get a higher education. Maybe in the halls of higher learning he would find motivation, ambition and a calling in life. Jake accepted their advice even though he had no ambitions and wasn't sure how he would answer life's call if it came to him. He enrolled in college and assumed that life's path would become self-evident in the next four years without any conscious effort on his part. He was content to let fate shape his life.

That easy-going complacent attitude hit a snag early in the first semester when Jake met with his faculty adviser, Dr. Julian Ripley. Ripley told Jake that all students matriculating in the college had to choose a major—some course of study that would lead to a meaningful career. He then launched into a long-winded lecture about the importance of serious career planning, the value of carefully weighing all options, and the rewards that come from making an informed decision. Jake remembered that he was completely taken aback by this unexpected requirement. In the past he simply picked vocations that he thought were different, possibly glamorous, and might prove interesting, but he never gave any thought to whether they were practical or even reasonable considerations. Up to that moment he'd never thought about what he really wanted to do in life.

He assumed that when he went to college and took an assortment of courses, everything would come together and a career field would just evolve into being. Jake was content to let the college education process shape his career path. Now he was told that it was his responsibility to choose a career, and to his chagrin he found that he was totally unprepared to do that.

He went home and looked through the college catalog. He evaluated the many subjects offered in the catalog carefully considering each as a possible course of study and hoping that some subject would leap out and capture his imagination. After two hours of thumbing back and forth through the pages of the catalog, Jake realized that nothing interested him. He had no ambition and he didn't want to be or do anything. In the end, he decided to major in political science, not because he liked the subject, but because nothing else appealed to him and political science seemed like a subject that offered a modicum of interest without requiring much effort or commitment.

The next day Jake met with his faculty adviser and declared his choice of a major field of study. The man was pleased with Jake's selection. He pointed out that political science would provide an excellent foundation for a career in politics or law. Jake listened to the man's comments but was less than enthusiastic. Secretly he loathed the idea of going into either field, but he tried not to show his indifference. Jake simply smiled and thanked the man for his counsel and departed. Inwardly nothing his adviser said had effect on him because Jake didn't believe a word of what Ripley said.

During the next four years in college, Jake studied political science. He took the required courses and added a few electives. He passed all his subjects and got good grades but his interest was minimal—nothing captured his imagination. He simply went through the motions toward graduation assuming that the college curriculum would shape his future.

Thus, without realizing it, Jake was simply allowing the nebulous forces of fate to come together and guide him through life without any conscious effort on his part. He went through four years of college avoiding making positive decisions and simply taking the easiest, least complicated path to follow—much like following the path on a board game trusting that it will lead to the winning square.

When Jake graduated from college, he still had no idea of what he wanted to do with the rest of his life. He knew that he didn't want to go to graduate school or law school. In fact, didn't feel like doing much of anything, but he knew that he had to get a job and earn a salary to pay the rent, buy food and purchase clothing. *What to do?*

He went on the Internet and half-heartedly searched the job market for employment opportunities. He had no specific goal in mind, and his qualifications for any career were meager so the pickings were slim and his choices limited. Forced by the necessities of life and a rapidly diminishing savings account, he accepted a job in The Yankee Standard Company, a company that manufactured porcelain fixtures: toilet bowls, urinals, and bidets—not exactly glamorous products.

It was a five-day-a-week office job. He reported to work at nine am and departed at five. The work was not especially demanding or interesting, but it was something to do and he earned an adequate salary. Each day in the office, he took orders from builders, contractors and project developers for toilet bowls, urinals, and bidets. He processed the orders and had the factory ship the products to building sites all over the world. Jake mused that his job entailed putting fixtures in place so people could shit and piss all over his work. It was a mundane and boring job but somebody had to do it and he earned enough money to eat and pay the rent.

He never had much enthusiasm for the job nor for the company. The one pursuit that he did enjoy was working out at the health club in his neighborhood. At first, he only went to the club on Saturday afternoons. Then he started going one or two evenings after work. Very soon he became a gym rat going to the health club every day for at least an hour but often for two or three hours.

At that point he found a small spark of ambition and he actually made a career choice, albeit a minor one. He took a certification course and became a personal trainer. He said goodbye to the world of toilet fixtures and to The Yankee Standard Company and he became a full-time personal trainer. It was a job with limited benefits and not much in the way of career potential, but Jake liked doing it. And for the time being, that was all that mattered to him.

In less than a year, he attracted a number of clients and developed a steady business. That is how he met Karen Pointer.

In the beginning, Karen was simply a client that he trained to keep in shape. She had a pretty face, sexy figure and a vivacious personality. She was fun to be around and they worked well together. Soon their relationship changed from professional to personal, from trainer-client to friends to lovers. It wasn't long before she moved into his apartment and they started living together. All went well for the first couple of years.

During that time, Karen had a minor administrative position with a large public relations firm on Park Avenue South. As far as Jake could tell she was competent in her job and liked her work and she seemed content to be in her current position. But then she started associating with another class of people in the firm—people who talked about moving up in the company, seeking greater responsibility, and seizing the levers of corporate power. They convinced her that she should go to business school to get an MBA.

She told Jake of her desire to go to graduate school. He was agreeable to her ambition, and said that he would support her while she was in school. So, he worked and she studied, and she got her MBA in record time. Fortified with her MBA, she was able to move up the echelons of the corporate administration to assume greater responsibility, power and importance, and she came to believe that getting ahead was the most important goal in life.

At that point she was ready to return the favor that he had bestowed. She announced that she would work and support Jake while he went back to school. The only problem was that he didn't want to go back to school. He was perfectly content being a personal trainer. Karen urged him to quit the gym and go to graduate school or law school, but he refused, maintaining that he was happy doing what he was doing.

After that admission, Karen began to see Jake in a different light and that caused a rift in their relationship. She felt that with his improvident attitude he would never amount to anything. She felt that he would always be a loser and she told him so. The rift widened and festered in the following months and their relationship turned from hot passion to cold indifference. It wasn't long before she moved out to seek greener pastures. Jake stayed in his apartment and continued to work as a personal trainer.

Now, however, Jake began to rethink his attitude. Until now, he never gave much thought to his future. He had always been content to take life as it unfolded with no concern as to what the next year would bring. He remembered that his parents and teachers told him that his cavalier attitude was irresponsible and that he had to take command of his life. He should find a goal and work toward it. It was essential that he find a greater purpose in life.

He had always dismissed that advice, but after Karen left he began to ask himself if maybe he had been wrong all along. At that point Jake thought that maybe it was time to change his ways and look for something to give his life a greater sense of meaning. The problem was that he didn't know where to look for that meaning. *How do you find purpose when you have spent your life avoiding it?*

CHAPTER 2

Soon after that, Jake met Drake Perry and a pivotal point in his life began to take shape—although he was unaware of it at the time. Perry started as one of Jake's clients. Jake didn't know anything about Perry. He only knew that Perry came to the gym and trained under his supervision three times a week for hourly workout sessions. After their workouts, they would often go down to the salad bar in the club, munch rabbit food together and chat. Their initial conversations were casual, touching on a variety of subjects: politics, sports, movies, food, and women.

These conversations seemed innocuous to Jake, but there was a subtle purpose behind Perry's easygoing conversational manner. Perry casually steered their discussions to focus on Jake. He asked Jake about his background—where he grew up, where he went to school, his opinions and his ambitions.

Jake admitted that he really didn't have much ambition and he never thought much about a career. He said that until recently he was content with being a physical trainer, but he confessed that now he wished that he could find something else—something that would give him a greater sense of purpose and direction in life. He expressed a desire to find a job that would be challenging, utilize more of his abilities and give him a feeling that his efforts made a difference.

Jake didn't know it at the time, but Drake Perry worked for The Bureau of Research and Information Acquisition or BRIA—a bland and innocuous title if ever there was one.

Actually, BRIA was anything but bland. It was an espionage agency much like the CIA but whereas the CIA spied on foreign insurgents, BRIA confined its operations to the United States. BRIA investigated and gathered information on any group or organization that was suspected of clandestine activity or espionage within the United States. In this respect, BRIA was much like the FBI, but there was one important difference. The FBI worked within the letter of the law. FBI agents obtained the necessary warrants before conducting a search. They got court orders before seizing property. In other words, they played by the rules.

The agents at BRIA observed no such niceties. They secretly broke into offices, opened safes and files, copied or took what they wanted and searched premises to find weapons or materials. Their motto was: *Do what it takes, but don't get caught.* Needless to say, BRIA was not an organization that anyone in the federal government wanted to acknowledge. When it was set up, it was designed to be an obscure organization buried under echelons of bureaucracy—an organization within an office within a sub-department attached to a higher department connected to a federal branch that was an adjunct of another branch buried under an umbrella of obscure federal titles. It was a masterpiece of Byzantine government obfuscation.

Most people—even those working in high government positions— had never heard of BRIA and were totally unaware of its existence. The few people who might have heard of BRIA assumed that it was a just another boring office of pencil-pushing, white-collar statisticians and nerds in the alphabet bureaucracy of the federal system; simply a research-and-information-gathering department—although what research and what information was anybody's guess. No one bothered to ask and no one volunteered any information.

All of the people who worked at BRIA were dedicated to the ideals of American democracy. True, they often broke the rules and frequently worked outside the letter of the law, but they truly believed that they were working for a higher, noble cause—the safety and security of the United States. That to accomplish these objectives, the ends justified the means.

And, in fact, their devious methods did get results; BRIA was able to put an end to many nefarious, clandestine activities and eliminate a number of subversive organizations that threatened the security of the United States and possibly could have undermined the very fabric of American democracy. Moreover, BRIA was able to accomplish these objectives without getting bogged down in a lot of bureaucratic or judicial red tape. Those few people who knew about BRIA and its methods were aware that it was a devious, but highly effective organization, and were reluctant to interfere with its methods.

Drake suspected that Jake might be a good field agent and he surreptitiously probed to see if he might bring Jake into the organization. That was how BRIA got most of its employees and all of its field agents—through personal contacts. After all, BRIA couldn't very well place an ad on the Internet looking for people who were willing to disregard the law and break into offices and buildings in the middle of the night to gather information. No, recruitment had to be more innocuous and calculated.

During their conversations, Perry shrewdly shaped their dialogues to subtly introduce Jake to world of intelligence gathering, but without going into the specifics—he didn't speak about the clandestine part of the work—about breaking into places or bending the law to collect data. Instead, he described the work as an office job that was fascinating, topical and often lucrative. When he felt that he had sufficiently aroused Jake's interest, Perry mentioned that there was a part-time job available at BRIA and if Jake took it, he could earn some extra money. Jake was intrigued by the prospect and figured, *what the hell! Maybe this is the opportunity that I've been looking for, so why not give it a try?*

The next day he met Perry and they went to the BRIA office which was located in an antiseptic, nondescript glass and steel office building on Sixth Avenue in midtown Manhattan. Jake learned that he would be working in *Information Acquisitions*. The job seemed simple and straight forward; Jake was handed a small pile of folders that contained news briefs, statistical data, facts and figures, files, and assorted information items about companies and organizations in the United States.

Jake had to read through all the items and put them together into a meaningful report. It seemed easy enough, and he applied himself with diligence and industry and wrote competent reports. But after sifting through the information and writing a few reports, Jake noticed something peculiar—often the facts and figures that he sifted through revealed the inner workings and secret operations within private organizations. He saw, for instance, that one company had undercover dealings with a foreign terrorist organization. Another company had been secretly smuggling arms and munitions into the United States.

This appeared to be underground information that was not accessible from traditional news sources. And Jake wondered how BRIA came by this stuff.

He expressed his concerns to Drake Perry.

"Drake," he began, "I've been writing a couple of reports and I noticed something strange."

"What's that?"

Jake told Perry about the facts he found information, about terrorists and secret armaments.

Then he asked, "Drake, where is BRIA getting this stuff from? After all this isn't something that you find in annual reports or on the evening news. This is really secret stuff and it seems to me that these companies would go to great lengths to keep all their dealings under wraps. They certainly would not want the public to know about their dirty laundry. So, how did we get it?"

Perry smiled with satisfaction. This was the moment that he had been waiting for—the moment when Jake Barrada's curiosity was aroused and his interest was captured. Perry leaned forward and he explained what really went on in BRIA. He told Jake that BRIA was an internal spy organization. He described how it employed covert agents to enter the premises of suspicious organizations under the cover of darkness and the methods these agents used to acquire any and all information that might be useful for its purposes.

Jake listened to all of this with interest. When Perry paused, he asked, "Yeah, but isn't this what the FBI is for? Isn't it supposed to capture the bad guys?'

"Sort of," replied Perry, "but the Bureau plays it safe. They follow the letter of the law."

"And BRIA doesn't?" asked Jake.

Perry shook his head. Then he went on to explain to Jake that laws, rules and regulations were blatantly ignored in the interest of the safety and security of the United States. It was risky, and sometimes dangerous work—but operatives had the satisfaction of knowing that they nailed the bad guys who were trying to undermine the United States of America. Moreover, the agents relished the risks and took pride in knowing that they were keeping America safe.

Perry tried to make the job sound as mysterious, intriguing, tantalizing, and patriotic as possible. His was a cleverly calculated spiel to capture Jake's imagination, stimulate his curiosity, arouse his taste for risk and adventure and at the same time appeal to his love of country. As he was telling all of this, Drake studied Jake's face for any reaction. When he saw that he had aroused Jake's interest and piqued his curiosity, Perry offered him the opportunity to venture out into the field of covert operations.

"What about you Jake? Is this something that you think you'd like to get a piece of?"

The whole idea seemed far-fetched to Jake. It was like something out of a graphic adventure novel, but it captured Jake's imagination. He wondered what it would be like to be a combination spy, intelligence agent and cat burglar. This seemed like a once-in-a-lifetime opportunity to do something meaningful, to go beyond the confines of the everyday work world, and at the same time to experience the thrill of risk-taking. It seemed like a chance to venture into clandestine adventure and to move closer to the edge of life. Maybe this was the opportunity to do something meaningful in his life—to acquire a sense of purpose that had always eluded him. His gut told him to go for it.

"Okay," said Jake, "I'm probably crazy but I'll give it a try. How do we go about it."

"We pay a visit to *Operations* and see what assignments are in the works. Then we ask how you can get in on it."

"Is *Operations* in this building?" asked Jake.

Perry shook his head. "No. This is only *Information Acquisitions. Operations* is in a totally different building on the Westside. Let's meet here on Monday at ten. Then we'll go downtown together and I'll show you the complete setup."

Monday morning came around and Jake met Drake Perry in front of the office building on Sixth Avenue. They walked across the street and took the subway to Union Square and walked east on 14th street.

Jake was excited about going to the super-secret organization that was BRIA. He imagined that they were going to a gleaming, modern building with a glamorous facade and an interior with high-tech furnishings and state-of-the-art equipment. As they were walking, Jake's excitement was mounting because he knew that in a few minutes they would come to a sleek government building, the headquarters of BRIA, the master spy organization.

They got to 10th Avenue, turned right and walked two blocks North. Jake couldn't believe his eyes when they arrived at their destination. It was a drab, non-descript building with a dirt-encrusted, black brick facade. The windows were coated with thick grime that made them opaque. On the street level there was a garage entrance fortified with a drop-down, battered steel door that was pitted with corrosion, had extensive dents and painted with a montage of obscure calligraphy and primitive graffiti. A few feet beyond was the entrance door, a weathered, locked, metal door which had a motley surface of peeling paint and scabs of red-brown rust. Above the entrance door was a sign: *United Warehouse Facilities*. From all outside appearances it looked like a run-down building that was dilapidated, lifeless, and totally deserted.

Jake was clearly surprised and disappointed. It wasn't at all what he expected.

"Is this it?" he asked. "Is this dump the main headquarters of BRIA?"

Perry smiled at Jake's disappointment. "Yeah, this is it. Surprised? Not what you imagined is it? Well, hold your comments until you get inside."

Perry moved to the entrance door. It had a doorknob with a digital-combination key lock. Perry glanced around to see if there were any pedestrians nearby. There was nobody. He turned his attention to the door lock and punched in a series of numbers. The lock clicked and he rotated the knob to open the door. The two men stepped inside to a small, dingy lobby dimly lit by four bare bulbs. They paused to acclimate their eyes to the dim light.

Jake looked around and scrutinized the room. The walls and floor of the lobby were dirty. It looked like they hadn't been cleaned in years. Some of the floor tiles were broken revealing the wooden subfloor underneath. The entire place was dim, dirty, neglected and in utter disrepair. The room had a smell of stale urine.

"Hell!" exclaimed Jake. "This place stinks. It's a shit pit. Do people actually work here?"

Perry grinned at Jake's discomfort. "You're about to see. We have to go up to the first floor."

Jake looked to the elevator and to his chagrin, he saw a sign saying that the elevator was out of order.

Perry anticipated Jake's next comment. "Yeah! We're gonna have to walk up. But it's only one flight, and we're in good shape. That's what we go to the gym for."

They entered the stairwell and started climbing. The stairwell was narrow, dim, fetid, and hot. Jake was sweating when he reached the first floor and he was beginning to regret ever coming to BRIA.

On the first floor there was another grubby door much like the street-entrance door. Perry went through the keypad ritual and opened the door. They stepped into a vestibule and encountered another door. This door was markedly different from the previous two. It was of polished steel; absent were the doorknob and combination-key pad. Instead there was a metal slot that accepted ID cards. Next to slot was an electronic pad for palm recognition and above that was a scanner with a glass panel for face recognition. Perry inserted his ID card then went through the palm and face recognition procedure. A series of beeps indicated that his identity was verified and the steel door slid open.

Perry retrieved his ID and the two men stepped through the doorway into a different world. It was a dazzling, busy, high-tech office. Gone were the dirt and grime, the foul smells, the dim lighting, the broken floor tiles, and the deserted, lifeless atmosphere. Here was a large office complex, brightly lit, with a polished floor, clean-painted walls, desks, partitions, stainless steel, and glass. It was an environment active with a multitude of people. Some were technologists working in front of computer screens, others were clustered in small groups engaged in hushed, intense discussion and still others working in offices behind closed doors analyzing data and planning projects and operations. This was a super-scientific, electronic environment with state-of-the-art equipment for communication, surveillance, hacking, and confidential, sophisticated cyber activity.

Jake looked around, taking in every detail of this polished environment and he was amazed at the transformation. Now this was more like what he had first imagined. Perry stood by and said nothing but he smiled as he saw the wonderment on Jake's face.

"Is this more like what you were expecting?" Perry asked.

Jake nodded. "I can't believe the difference. Outside this place looks like a rundown dump, but inside it's…well, it's different. Really different!"

"You can't run a big, hush-hush organization like this in the heart of the city without camouflage. The dirt and grime hide us from curious eyes. Go over and take a look out the window."

Jake was hesitant to go over to the window because he knew the window was covered with accumulated soot, dirt and grime. He didn't expect to see anything, but urged on by Perry he walked to a nearby window. Jake looked out, and to his surprise he found that he could see the cityscape outside. He glanced down the street below. It was much the same as when he came into the warehouse; the sidewalk was deserted and only a few passing vehicles moved along the avenue.

Jake turned back to Perry. "I don't get it. From the street it looks like the windows are coated with an inch of black muck. You can't see through them, but from here I can see outside to the street. How is that possible?"

Perry smiled. "The exterior surface of the window is coated with a film of fine-engineered particles that look like dirt and grime from the outside. From the street the windows are opaque; nobody can see inside. But from the inside, the windows are transparent and the people inside can look through the high-tech coating to see the outside world.

This stuff was created by our *Research and Development* department. Clever huh?

"Okay, let's go over to *Operations*. There's someone I want you to meet."

With Perry leading the way they walked to a corner office. The door was open and a man was seated behind a desk working at a computer. Perry knocked on the door frame to capture the man's attention. When the man looked up, Perry entered the office and said, "Morning Phil, this is the guy I was telling you about, Jake Barrada. Jake thinks that he'd like to become a field agent. Jake this is Phil Niekrom. Phil is one of the special operations supervisors."

The two men murmured greetings and shook hands.

"Okay," said Perry, "I'll leave you guys to talk. I've got other work to do." Then he exited leaving Jake and Niekrom alone in the office.

Niekrom spoke, "How much did Drake tell you about what we do here?"

Jake shrugged. "Not much. He said that BRIA tackles jobs that the FBI can't. He made it sound like you guys operate like burglars and sneak thieves entering places in the middle of the night, bending rules and even breaking the law."

Niekrom smiled. "Yeah, that's vaguely correct—in a nutshell. And even though we do bend some rules we're careful not to step too far over the line. We don't kill people or beat anyone up.

"Basically, when intelligence sources find a suspicious target that needs further investigation—undercover snooping—they contact BRIA. When we get the case, we scrutinize the target and *Strategic Planning* puts together a plan of operation. The plan is handed to an operations supervisor, like me. I go over the plan then call in one of our field agents. All our field agents are freelancers—independent contractors if you like. The two of us review the plan together and try to work out the bugs and drawbacks. Then we talk about payment. Most of our assignments are simple one-night entry jobs so the price is already set. Some jobs are more complicated and may require special equipment or more than one night to complete. These pay more.

"If the agent agrees to do the job—he can turn it down if he wants—we set up a date and time to go ahead. That's when he goes into the geek's den and gets the evidence—if there is any to be gotten—then he takes a powder leaving no trace behind."

"What happens if he gets caught in the act?" asked Jake.

"Depends on who catches him. If it's the local cops, they arrest him and take him to the nearest police station. He'll be allowed a phone call, and he will call our lawyer, J.J. Detwilder. That's John Jonah Detwilder. He's one of our guys. He's top notch and he'll pull strings and push levers to get the charges dropped."

"Suppose your man gets caught by the enemy?"

"Ah!" replied Niekrom, "then it can get dicey. Remember, the geeks we're spying on are playing hardball. They don't take kindly to guys breaking into their lair and snooping around to find evidence that might throw a monkey wrench into their business or land them in jail. They'll do whatever it takes to keep their operations undercover—even if it means eliminating a nosey intruder."

"Have you lost men doing these operations?"

Niekrom nodded. "A couple. In the last four years we've run over five hundred missions. In that time, we lost two men. They went into the enemy camp and didn't come out. We never found out what happened to them. Considering the number of missions we ran and the bunch of guys involved, two losses isn't bad. But that's a small concoliation to the two guys who never came back."

Jake grimaced at the remark.

Niekrom picked up on Jake's expression and continued. "Look, I know my attitude sounds callous and indifferent, but this is a war we're fighting. There are no tanks, or planes or cannons, but we're still up against ruthless geeks who want to wreck the United States. And even though we try to do everything possible to anticipate the hazards and minimize the risks, there are bound to be some casualties along the way. Agents go into a mission knowing that they might not come back. What all this amounts to is that when all is said and done, it's up to each agent to peel his own banana."

Niekrom looked at Jake to see how his words were registering. He gave Jake a minute to reflect on everything that he said. Then he asked, "Well, Jake I've just given you a capsule sketch of what the job is all about. Are you still interested?"

Jake didn't answer immediately. Instead, he thought about all Niekrom had said, and he tried to consider what was involved and what he might be required to do. He had to ask himself, *did he really want to do this kind of work?* All his life he had avoided the responsibility of choosing any kind of career path. He always assumed that a career path would unexpectedly appear and a job would fall into his lap. Now it seemed that is exactly what has happened. Jake sensed that opportunity was knocking and he decided to answer the call.

"Yeah," he said to Niekrom, "I want to go for it."

"Good!" replied Niekrom. "Consider yourself part of the organization."

CHAPTER 3

"Suppose I tell you about an assignment that we're about to put into play. That will give you a clearer picture of what we do and how we work."

Jake leaned forward in anticipation as Niekrom opened a desk draw and pulled out a manila envelope with a label marked Secret. When Jake saw the label on the envelope he sat upright.

"Wait a minute," Jake cried.

"What's the matter?" asked Niekrom.

"The label says *Secret.*"

"Yeah! So?"

"Well, don't I need a background check and a security clearance before I can look at that stuff?"

Niekrom smiled. "You already have your security clearance, and the background check was completed months ago." He opened a desk drawer and pulled out a file folder. He tossed it across the desk in front of Jake. "Here! Have a gander at this. See yourself as others see you."

Jake picked up the folder. It was almost an inch thick. As he randomly read through the document, he was amazed at the amount of information, facts, details and minutiae that were packed in the pages. This wasn't just a dossier; it was more like a biography that recorded Jake's life history.

The first page was about where and when Jake was born and items about his parents and relatives. The following pages described all the places that he had lived and where he went to school. He looked at his school record and was amused to find that there was a paragraph about his experience in Mrs. Meehan's sixth grade class and the essay he wrote expressing his dream of becoming a drunken sea captain.

Jake skimmed through other pages and saw a record of his past life and how he came to be the person he is. It was fascinating material. He wanted to read more, but he knew that Niekrom was waiting patiently for him to finish so they could get on with the upcoming mission. Jake closed the folder, put it back on the desk and looked up.

"Satisfied?" asked Niekrom.

"Yeah! I can't believe that you guys found out all this stuff about me. I mean all the details. Who put this together? How did they find out all this information? When did they do the search?"

"The *when* part is easy. When Drake Perry started training with you in the gym, he thought that you might have what it takes to become a field agent, he contacted *Background Investigations* and suggested that they to run a background check on you. That's the *who*. As to *how*, I can't answer that. I only know that the guys in *Background* are good at what they do and they can find out information about you that you've probably forgotten about.

"Okay, now suppose we get down to brass tacks and go over the mission."

He picked up the manila envelope, extracted the contents and laid them out across the desk. Most of the pages were printed text. There were also some diagrams and floor plans and a few photographs.

"Okay," began Niekrom, "the plan for this assignment was put together by *Strategic Planning*. The objective is a shipping company, Tabor Import & Export. It's somewhere in the Bronx, but you don't have to know exactly where—a van will take you there and bring you back."

Niekrom picked up one of the photos. "From the outside, Tabor Import & Export appears to be a legit company that ships furniture, textiles, ceramics, and fine art from Asia into the United States. However, intelligence sources suspect that there is more to Tabor Import & Export than fine art, furniture and textiles.

"Intelligence believes that this company is a front for an extensive smuggling operation that brings arms, weapons and explosives into the United States. Once in the country, the contraband ordinance is distributed to terrorists, agent provocateurs, and radical extremists to stir up trouble, challenge local law enforcement services, promote civil unrest and erode confidence in the internal security of the United States.

"The problem is that there is no hard evidence to back up these suspicions. BRIA was called in to find that evidence. *Strategic Planning* studied the problem and created the blueprint for the operation. Code name for this mission is *Operation Silk Worm*. The plan is simple enough. One of our agents will sneak into the joint after hours and nose around and try and dig up proof that *Tabor Import & Export* is running a smuggling and terrorist operation. The field agent that I've chosen for this mission is a guy named Tork."

"Tork! Is that his name?"

"That's the name he goes by. All our field agents use a one-name moniker. They don't use last names. You can use your own name or pick something else, but it's gotta be short and simple."

"I'll stick with *Jake*."

"Suit yourself. Tork will be in charge of the mission. Jake, you'll go along to assist and learn from him."

"Will I need any training or special equipment for this job?"

"Nope. You're just going in to search files and take pictures. The only equipment you'll need is a camera. Tork will give you that and he'll carry the rest. It's really a no-brainer. Well, that's about it. Any questions?"

"Yeah! When and where will I meet Tork?"

"Wednesday morning at ten am. You'll meet here and he'll go over any details that I haven't covered.

"Now go down to the ground floor and visit *Payroll*. They'll give you a six-digit identification number that you'll use when you submit your invoices. They'll ask you how you want to get your check—by mail, direct deposit, or hold for pick-up. After you finish with them, go across the hall to *Identification*. They'll take your photo, do a palm and face scan, cut you an ID card and give you the numerical code for the front door.

"When you finish with them you can go home. But come back here on Wednesday morning at ten to hook up with Tork. That's all for now. Welcome to BRIA, Jake."

The two men stood up and shook hands. Then Jake went downstairs to find *Payroll* and *Identification*. When he finished in those departments, he went home.

Back in his apartment, he opened a can of beer and sat down to reflect on all that had just happened. He had just joined an undercover organization and was about to take on a mysterious and possibly exciting career. For the first time in his life, Jake truly felt like he had acquired a true purpose—it looked like he was about to begin an exciting adventure with challenges, risks and possibly danger. This would be a test of his courage, imagination and his abilities. Maybe he would be up to it, and then again maybe not—time and circumstance would tell, but for now he was looking forward to his first night of true adventure.

The next day, Tuesday, Jake was back in the gym and resumed his work as a personal trainer. He had three clients; one in the morning, the next in the afternoon, and the third in the early evening. He put each of his clients through their paces doing stretches, bends, calisthenics, weight training, and some aerobics. He had a feeling of satisfaction from helping these people maintain physical fitness, while at the same time there was the thought churning in the back of his mind that he was about to gain a deeper gratification when he tackled his first mission in the clandestine world of espionage. He was about to add another dimension to his lifestyle, and he wondered how it would all turn out.

On Wednesday morning, Jake took the subway to 14th street and walked to the grimy noir fortress that was BRIA headquarters. He stood before the entrance door and punched in the series of numbers on the digital-combination lock. He had a brief moment of hesitation when he gripped the door knob because he wondered if he had hit the right numbers in the correct sequence and if the door would open. He twisted the knob and the door opened. So far, so good. Jake walked into the rancid lobby and he smiled as he recalled the feeling of revulsion that he had when he first stepped into this foul place. The room was still a sludge pit, but now Jake had the secret knowledge that on the other side of these squalid walls were polished offices occupied by elite specialists conducting the business of clandestine law enforcement. Moreover, he knew that he was about to become part of that exclusive corps of operatives.

Jake climbed the stairs to the second floor and went through the identification process to get access to the inner offices. Then he walked to the corner office where found Phil Niekrom seated behind his desk. When he appeared in the doorway, Niekrom stood up and greeted him.

"Morning Jake. You're right on time. Unfortunately, Tork will be late. He phoned to say that he's trapped in a subway that's stalled due to a police action. He should be in presently. Why don't you go up to the cafeteria on the third floor and grab yourself a cup of coffee? You might want to take this case folder with you so you can read about *Operation Silk Worm* while you're waiting. I'll send Tork up as soon as he gets here."

"How will he know which one is me?"

"Don't worry, I'll tell him to look for the guy in the green shirt sitting alone and reading a case folder. How many people in the cafeteria will fit that description?"

Jake went up to the cafeteria, sat at an empty table and opened the file on *Operation Silk Worm*. About a half hour later a man walked into the cafeteria. He looked around at the few people in the cafeteria then headed straight for Jake. Jake looked up at the man coming toward him. The guy was tall. He looked physically fit, alert and self-assured. Jake knew intuitively that this was Tork, the field operative that he was going to work with.

Jake stood up when Tork came to the table. They shook hands, murmured vague greetings and sat down.

"Phil said that he filled you in on *Operation Silk Worm* so you know the score."

Jake nodded. "He didn't tell me when we are supposed to do the job."

"Right! We go in this coming Saturday night. On missions like this it's best to go in on the weekends 'cause there's less chance of anyone working late in the office."

"Where and when do we meet?"

"We'll meet at midnight on the upper East side on Third and Sixty-fifth. There's a work scaffold on the West side of the street. We'll meet under that. Try to be there between eleven forty-five and five minutes after the hour. We'll exchange cell phone numbers so we can call each other in case we get delayed. When we meet I'll call for a van to pick us up. It will take us to the Bronx."

"What should I wear?"

"Good question! Wear sneakers or rubber-soled shoes. Dark clothes … dark jeans … black ones if you have them…and a dark shirt. Oh here, I got this for you."

Tork reached into a shoulder bag that he was carrying. He pulled out a black baseball cap and tossed it on the table in front of Jake.

"I got this for you from *Supply*. You can wear it this coming Saturday. Oh, and Jake, smile. Who knows but this might be fun!"

Jake tried to smile, but he had his doubts.

On the night of the operation, Jake arrived at the rendezvous spot ten minutes before midnight. He looked around and saw that the area was deserted with no one in sight. At midnight on the dot Tork showed up and they greeted each other with low grunts. Both men were wearing dark clothes, sneakers, and dark baseball caps. Tork pulled out his cell phone and made a brief call then he turned to Jake.

"I just called the van for a pick up. He said that he's nearby and should be here in about five minutes."

Jake nodded but said nothing.

The two men waited under the scaffold for five minutes, then a black van pulled up to the curb. Tork opened the side door and he and Jake climbed inside. Tork pulled the door shut, the van pulled away and headed up the Avenue. Tork and Jake were in the back seat of the van so Jake could only see the back of the driver's head and since there were no side windows in the vehicle, Jake couldn't follow the route they were taking to their destination.

They drove in silence; the three men understood that there was no need for dialogue, thus no one said a word. Tork sat perfectly still, maintaining an attitude of calm, cool composure. Jake tried to mimic that iron-nerved posture but inwardly he was churning with excitement knowing that he was about to tackle an exploit that was more daring than anything he had ever attempted in his life. After about forty-five minutes the van pulled up to a curb on a street in the Bronx and stopped.

As Tork rose to the side door, he said to the driver, "I'll call you later for the pick-up."

The driver raised his hand in acknowledgement and Tork opened the door and stepped out onto the sidewalk with Jake close behind. Tork closed the van door and the vehicle sped away and disappeared around the corner leaving both men standing on the sidewalk of a deserted street. It was after midnight and all was dark and all was quiet.

Jake had studied photos of the Tabor Import & Export building days before, but now, as he looked about, nothing looked familiar.

"Is this it?" he asked.

"No, our objective is two blocks away, but it's better if we approach it on foot. There could be a cop patrol car or a night watchman working outside, and two men getting out of a black van in the middle of the night in front of the warehouse might look suspicious. We'll walk the rest of the way looking like a couple of guys coming home from working the night shift somewhere."

They walked in silence, but before they got to the end of the second block, Tork halted.

"Okay, our target is on the next street to the left. When we get to the corner we'll look to the left. If we see anybody—anybody at all—we'll turn right and walk around the block. Got that?"

Jake nodded and they walked to the corner where they paused and looked to the left. The street was deserted. Jake recognized the building that he had seen in the operation file—this was their objective. They crossed the street, turned left and walked along the sidewalk adjacent to the building. They stopped at a solidary door.

Tork pulled a key out of his pocket and opened the door. They stepped inside closing the door behind them.

"How'd you get a key to this place?" asked Jake.

"A guy from *Reconnaissance* came by a couple of weeks ago. He took an impression of the lock and made this key. Having a key made beats standing outside in the middle of the night trying to pick the lock."

Jake marveled at how this entire operation had been carefully thought out and planned down to the smallest detail with various operatives coming forward, evaluating obstacles, providing transport and solving possible problems in advance, so the weight of execution didn't fall on any one individual.

The two men were inside a stairwell. They donned gloves, and Tork pulled out a light and scanned the interior walls, floor, steps and ceiling.

He spoke in hushed tones. "*Reconnaissance* checked out this well— they didn't find any bugs or surveillance eyes, but that was over a week ago. The geeks could have put something in place since then. So, I'm doing a quick check just to be sure."

During these few minutes, Jake stood by, waiting and watching, while Tork examined every detail of the stairwell. Then Tork announced, "Okay, it looks clean. Let's go up. The entrance is on the fifth floor. You up to climbing stairs?"

Jake nodded and together they mounted the stairs. On the fifth floor they encountered a door with a red sign that read, *Door is wired. Alarm will sound if opened.*

Jake wondered how they would get past this door without sounding the alarm, but he kept silent because he assumed that even this obstacle had been anticipated and a way had been found to get around it. He watched to see what Tork would do. Tork pulled a device out of his pack. It was a nondescript black box about the size of a cell phone and it had wires attached. The wires had magnetic disks on the ends. Tork positioned the disks to the door jamb and to the alarm box above the door.

"This gizmo will create a parallel alarm circuit so we can open the door without breaking the electrical signal from the door to the alarm. *O & E* made it. Let's see if it works."

Jake held his breathe while Tork gripped the door knob and slowly edged the door open. The alarm did not sound; the gizmo worked. Both men stepped through the doorway into a dimly-lighted hall. Tork turned around.

"I've got to rearrange the circuit wires to this side so I can shut door and disconnect the gizmo. We never leave our tracks behind." He disconnected and pocketed the gizmo, then said, "Okay, the office we want is down the hall."

They walked to the end of the hall and stopped before an office door. Tork pulled out another key and opened the door. They stepped inside the office and closed the door behind them.

Inside, Jake turned to Tork and said, "I'm amazed at how you know where to go and have everything you need and how all the details have been worked out."

"Yeah, *Reconnaissance* does all the leg work."

"How do they do it?"

"Beats the hell out of me. I think some of them come in like rats in the night. Others come in during the day posing as fire inspectors, insurance salesman, fuller brush men, or goofballs looking for the men's room. All I know is that they get their job done, so we can do ours.

"Okay, we gotta get a move on. Put on your head lamp and look through those file cabinets over there."

"What am I looking for?"

"Anything and everything that might show that these geeks are smuggling arms and bombs into the U.S. Here's a camera. If you come across anything suspicious take pictures of it. If in doubt, photo it."

After about a half-hour of searching files and desk drawers, Tork asked, "You got anything?"

"I got this shipping form that says *50 mm hardware from China.* That mean anything?"

"It might, but it's not enough. Okay, we've done all we can here. Close all the drawers and put everything back the way we found it, so no one will know we were here. Then we'll go down to the shipping room by the loading dock. It's just possible that we'll find some hard evidence down there."

The two men closed drawers and files and returned the office to the same condition that it was in when the entered. They stepped out into the hall and closed and locked the door behind them, then walked to the far end of the hall and took the service elevator to the ground level where they found the shipping room. The place was crowded with wooden packing crates.

"Okay," said Tork, "if we're gonna find anything, most likely it will be in one of these crates. Problem is that they all seem to be nailed shut. See if you can find one that's open so we don't have to make noise prying the lids off."

Jake and Tork examined a number of crates using their head lamps for illumination. Soon Jake said, "I found one that's open. The label says *Porcelain Vases.*"

They looked through the crate pulling out packing material and digging down between the vases. As they were doing this, Jake mused that he was back to handling porcelain, only this time it was vases and not toilet products.

"This is no good," said Tork. "It's only ceramic crap. Looks like we'll have to pry open one of the other crates."

"How we gonna do that?"

"I saw a crowbar on that worktable over there. That should do the trick." He walked to the worktable, grabbed the crowbar and looked around. "Let's try that crate over in the corner. It's out of the way and if we make noise it might not carry far."

They walked over to the crate. Tork examined the seams around the lid and nails securing it to the crate.

"I hope these nails aren't too long or it will be hell trying to pull them out. There's bound to be noise when I start prying this sucker up. Stay alert and keep your eyes peeled in case anyone comes in to investigate. If you see or hear anyone, douse your light and duck down behind the crate. Okay, here goes."

Tork forced the flat end of the crowbar in the narrow gap between the lid and the crate. He pushed down on the opposite end of the crow bar. There was a loud squawk as the lid came up from the crate. Tork paused.

"That was kinda loud. Anything? See anybody?"

"Nope, all is still. Nobody in sight."

"Okay, I'll tackle the other corners. Keep alert."

Tork went around pried up the other three corners and pulled the lid off. Then he looked down into the crate.

"What do we have here? Looks like a bunch of rugs."

"Yeah! The label says *Carpets from Turkey*."

"That's what it looks like. On the surface maybe, but there may be something underneath this crap. Let's dig deeper." Tork pulled back a couple layers of carpets and uncovered an assortment of military weaponry.

"Bingo! We hit pay dirt. These things look like some type of rocket launchers. And what do we have over here? Canisters of something. Could be gas, or incendiary bombs, or other explosives. Doesn't matter what. Let's take pictures of this stuff. Then we'll put the rugs back and replace the lid."

They put everything back in order and Tork replaced the lid.

"Okay," said Tork, "we got what we got what we came for. Let's get out of here. There's a door by the loading gate. We'll go out that way."

They walked to the door. Tork cracked it open and looked around to see if the coast was clear. It was; they exited the building and walked two blocks where Tork called the van for a pick-up. In less than an hour they were back in Manhattan.

CHAPTER 4

After they parted, Jake went back to his apartment. He made a small snack and opened a can of beer. He sat down at his kitchen table and while he sipped the beer and munched, he thought about all that he had done in the dead of night. Only a few hours ago, working alongside Tork, they broke into a suspicious building, bypassed alarm circuits, crept into forbidden territory, and penetrated an office where they searched and photographed secret files. Then they invaded the warehouse and opened crates. He remembered the emotional rush that he experienced when they discovered the contraband weapons. It was a night of adventure. It was all illegal, but he was one of the good guys so it was all right.

As he reflected on the night's activities, Jake realized that he relished the adventure, the risks, the potential dangers and the thrill that came from being an undercover agent. This was the first time in his life that he felt a real sense of accomplishment and purpose and this was the first time in his life that he felt that he was doing something meaningful. He was energized during every minute of the mission and he wanted to go out on another.

Two days later, Jake got a call from Phil Niekrom requesting that he come to his office. Jake went to Niekrom's office the following morning. Tork had already arrived and was sitting chatting with Niekrom.

"Morning Jake, said Niekrom. "Have a seat." Jake took up a chair next to Tork.

"I wanted to go over the results of your recent mission, *Operation Silk Worm*. The guys in *Strategic Planning* liked your pictures and your report. They sent them over to the FBI. The feds in the Bureau were impressed but they said that they couldn't move in on Tabor Import & Export because our evidence constitutes an illegal search. Not permissible in court."

"So, all our efforts went for nothing?" said Jake with disappointment. "It was a waste of time and all our work was a big zero?"

"Oh no! Quite the contrary," replied Niekrom. "*Strategic Planning* came up with another mission. You'll go back into Tabor Import & Export. Only this time you'll set fire to the joint."

Jake was dumbfounded. He looked back at Tork, unsure that he heard correctly. Tork said nothing but he had a slight smile on his face.

"Are you saying," asked Jake still unsure that he heard correctly, "that we're going to burn the building down?"

"No, nothing so drastic," replied Niekrom. "You just go in and start a blaze going—one that's hot enough and bright enough to get the fire department involved. The firemen come in and put out the blaze. But they suspect arson—which is right—so they bring in fire inspectors. Two of the fire inspectors will be FBI agents in disguise. They'll nose around and naturally they'll find the weapons and that's when the dung pile will sail into the oscillator and law and order will move in. Got the picture?"

"Sort of," said Tork. "What do we use to set the fire going? Matches and candles?"

"No, *Ordnance and Equipment* put together some sort of fire gizmos for you to work with. Someone from *O & E* is waiting for you on the fifth floor. Go up and see what they've devised."

Both men rose and started to exit the office, but Tork turned to Niekrom. "One question, chief," said Tork. "When do we go in?"

"Saturday night or Sunday. You pick whichever night works best for you."

Tork nodded and both men left the office, took the elevator up to the fifth floor and walked into a room. There was a man arranging some items on a table. They walked over to him.

Tork spoke, "Hello Oliver. Good to see you again. I want to introduce you to my partner. Oliver Vinick, this is Jake Barrada. Jake will be working with me on this assignment." The two men exchanged greetings. "Okay, Oliver show us what us what you boys in *O & E* have created. Wow us with your genius."

Oliver picked an item from the table and held it up. "This is the incendiary device that you'll be using. It's a fire bomb, that you will attach to the crates. We call them *hot potatoes*. You'll have twenty of them. They're loaded with hydroxyl-terminated polybutadiene. That's the same stuff that's used as solid fuel rocket propellant. It's a rubbery compound that binds the fuel and oxidizer together so when the device is activated it will create an instant hot blaze. That's just background info, you don't really have to know these details."

"That's good, one less thing on the final exam," said Tork somewhat sarcastically. Jake smiled at Tork's witticism, but Oliver seemed oblivious to Tork's attempt at levity.

Tork picked up one of the devices and examined it. "Tell us how these things work."

"Right! First you have to attach the device to the side of the crate. There's an adhesive pad on the back of each unit. Pull away this plastic backing film to expose the adhesive, then press the device firmly against the side of the crate—not more than half-way down. The adhesive should stick to any flat surface. If, for some reason, you find it doesn't stick, then there are screws recessed into the corners of the unit. Hold the device against the side of the crate and drive the screws home."

"What do we use to drive the screws?" asked Tork.

"This," said Oliver as he picked up another item from the table. "It's a ratchet screwdriver. You're probably familiar with these. Engage the tip of the screwdriver in the screwhead slots then press hard against the handle. The push will turn the screwdriver bit and drive the screw into the surface. These screws will penetrate wood, plastic, and soft metal. There are four screws—one in each corner—but for most surfaces, just two should do the trick.

"Okay, once the device is attached to the crate, pull up this antenna wire and push this black button on the side of the unit."

"Does that activate a timer on the device?" asked Tork.

"No, it only turns on the receiver that will capture the activation signal. That's what the antenna is for. It will pick up the activation signal."

"Where does the activation signal come from?" asked Jake.

Oliver picked up another item from the table. "From this! This unit is the transmitter. You only need one. It will broadcast the activation signal. Once all the *potatoes* are in place, stand in a central location and press this red button on the center of the transmitter then hold it up and wave it about. It will send an inaudible signal that will activate all the potatoes simultaneously."

"How much time between the activation signal and the moment when the *potatoes* ignite?"

"Fifteen minutes," replied Oliver. "When the *potato* is activated, a digital display panel will light up with red numbers, starting at fifteen minutes and counting down by the seconds to zero. At the zero moment the *potato* will burst into flame. Since they are all synchronized, they'll all ignite at the same time."

"Will there be an explosion?" asked Jake.

Oliver shook his head, "No, not likely, more like a loud fizz, as if you just opened a can of soda—although there will be twenty fizzes simultaneously, so that could make some noise but not a big bang. When these things ignite, the place will get hot and bright very quickly. I said that there's not going to be a big bang, but there may be explosives in some of the crates. When the fire hits them, there could be an explosion. In any case you'll want to get out and away before the flash point.

"Something else that I should mention…once these things are activated, there is no way to back track. You can't turn them off. So, make sure that you plan your getaway before pressing the activation signal. Get the picture?"

"Got it," said Tork. Jake nodded.

"Okay guys! That's it from me. You're on your own now. Have fun!" With that cheery comment, Oliver departed leaving Jake and Tork to look over the items assembled on the table. Both men picked up different units and examined them.

"Well," said Tork, "it looks pretty straight forward. We go into the building plant these gizmos on the crates, press the red button and get out before the place lights up."

"When do we go in?" asked Jake.

"Let's try for Saturday night. Then if something should happen to scuttle our plans, we still have Sunday to fall back on."

"Where do we meet? Here?"

Tork shook his head. "No, we'll meet in the same place as last time, under the scaffold on Third Avenue."

"Do we carry these things with us?"

"No," said Tork, "that could be awkward if the cops search our packs on the subway. These units will be in the pick-up van. When we get in the van we'll divvy them up, ten units each. I'll carry the transmitter."

"Well, I guess that's all we can do for now. Go home catch forty winks and meet me on Third Avenue around midnight on Saturday night."

With that said, Tork turned and walked away. Jake remained behind for a few minutes and looked over the various items on the table. This was a new wrinkle in the espionage game. Now they were not only going into the enemy encampment to sniff around, they were going in to do some real damage. Jake wondered what that would be like.

Early Saturday evening Jake was in his apartment. He had intended to rest up for the evening's mission but he was so charged with anticipation that he couldn't relax or nap. He put on his dark clothes and sneakers—which he called his adventure outfit—then he ate a snack and sat back in a chair contemplating the adventure that would come later in the night. He imagined that if all went according to plan, it would be a hot time in the Bronx. *What a way to spend Saturday night!*

Shortly after midnight Jake and Tork met under the scaffold. Five minutes later, the pick-up van arrived and took them to the drop-off place in the Bronx. They grabbed their packs, exited the van and walked two blocks to the side door of the Tabor Import & Export Company. Tork used the key to unlock the door; they entered the building and went straight to the shipping room.

"Okay," said Tork, "you take that side, I'll take this one. Let's see how fast we can place these gizmos and get outta here."

The two men separated and walked to the crates on opposite sides of the room. Jake pulled a *potato* from his backpack, ripped off the plastic backing film to expose the adhesive and pressed the unit in place on the side of a crate. The unit stuck firmly in place. He pulled up the antenna wire then moved on to mount another unit, then another, and another. In less than ten minutes he had all his *potatoes* mounted on the crates. He walked to the open center of the room where he met Tork.

"You placed all your *potatoes*?" asked Tork.

"Yeah!" said Jake. "Mine are all in place."

"Mine too! Okay let's get the show started and activate the units."

He pulled the transmitter from his backpack, pressed the red button and held the device overhead and waved it around.

"That should do it. We got fifteen minutes before the big fizz so let's make a quick run-around just to be sure that all the *potatoes* are activated"

Jake and Tork separated to return to their respective starting points. Each made a quick survey of their fire bombs. Jake saw that all his units were activated with the red digital numbers counting down to the ignition moment—fourteen minutes and forty-six seconds…forty-five seconds…forty-four seconds…forty-three seconds…

The two men came together in the center opening.

"Everything going on track?" asked Tork.

"Yeah," replied Jake. "The units are all in sync and counting down. Looks like we got about fourteen minutes plus change before the big burn. Now do we run?"

"Not yet. First, we gotta shut down the overhead sprinkler system."

"How we gonna do that?"

"There's a shutoff valve around here. It should be somewhere over in that direction." Tork used his flashlight to scan the far wall. He moved the beam around until it captured the target that he was looking for. "There it is, on that pipe running up the wall close to the exit door. Come on!"

Tork walked over to the pipe and gripped the wheel of the shutoff valve. He pulled hard and turned the wheel.

"Okay! That should do it. The sprinkler system is now deactivated."

"How did you know where this valve was?" asked Jake.

"*Reconnaissance*! Industrial buildings like this have to submit their fire prevention systems with the buildings department so, the fire inspectors can be sure everything is up to code. *Reconnaissance* went to the buildings department and checked out the plans."

Once again, Jake marveled at how various agents at BRIA moved to collect all the information and details necessary to execute the mission and insure that everything went smoothly without a hitch.

"Our work's done. Let's blow this joint. The exit door is over here."

Tork and Jake walked to the door. Tork pushed the crash bar to crack the door open. He peered out then quickly stepped back and quickly closed the door."

"What's the matter?" asked Jake.

"Cop patrol car coming down the street. We'll wait until it goes past so the cops don't see us coming out to make our getaway. We still got time to wait a minute or two for the coast to clear."

Jake looked around and saw the red display numbers on a nearby incendiary unit. The red numbers showed eleven minutes and fifty-three seconds. Ample time to wait for the street to get clear of witnesses.

They waited a few minutes then Tork cracked the door open and peeked out.

"Damn!" he said.

"'What's the matter now?" asked Jake.

"There's some drunk across the street, right in front of us. The cops have stopped to question him. Can you see one of the display timers on a potato so we know how many minutes we got before the big burn."

Jake looked around and saw the red numbers on a nearby timer.

"We got about ten minutes and a few seconds," said Jake.

"All right. There's still time. But let's hope the cops finish with this bum and get going so we can scram before the time runs out."

They stood by the door and waited a few more minutes, then Tork cracked the door open for another peek outside. He pulled it shut again.

"Double damn!" he said. "They're still at it. How long does it take to check out a drunk? How much time we got?"

"Six minutes and about seventeen seconds. Couldn't we try to get out another way?"

"I don't think so. The other doors may be wired and we haven't got much time for trial and error. Let's wait it out and hope the cops finish with the bum and move on."

They waited. Jake glanced over at the red numbers on the display timer of a nearby incendiary unit. Now the countdown was four minutes to flashpoint. A few moments passed and it was three minutes and fifty-three seconds. Jake was starting to get nervous, but Tork seemed indifferent to the fact that they were less than four minutes from being trapped in a room that was about to become an inferno.

Jake wondered, *how long could they continue to wait?*

Tork cracked open the door and peeked out. Then he pulled it shut again.

"Not yet," he murmured.

The red numbers were now at, two minutes and fifty-five seconds. Tork waited twenty seconds then peeked out.

"Okay!" he announced, "the coast is clear. Let's make our getaway. But no running. We'll try to walk nonchalantly across the street so as not to attract attention in case anyone is around."

Jake nodded. The two men exited the building and Tork pulled the door shut behind them. They walked casually across the street and headed down the street. They made two right turns which brought them around the block and back to face the building that they had just come out of. All was dark. All was quiet.

"I don't get it," said Jake, "it's been over two minutes since we got out of there but the windows are still dark. It looks like nothing has happened. Maybe the *potatoes* didn't go off."

"Maybe," said Tork, "but it could be that the fire's just getting started. It may take a few minutes before we see anything. Let's wait a bit to see if a blaze really gets going."

They stood across the street silently watching the building for any signs of change. They waited and watched. A few minutes went by and still there was no discernible change. Everything remained dark and quiet. It was beginning to look like the *hot potatoes* had failed and all their work had been in vain. Then suddenly Jake noticed an orange glow in one of the windows.

"It looks like there's a light in the window on the left."

"I see it," said Tork. "The other windows are starting to light up. Looks like the fire has started and it's spreading through the warehouse." Suddenly there was a small explosion. "Okay, that's got it. It sounds like some of the ammo caught fire and exploded. Well, we've done our job. There's a fire call box across on the other side of the street. Let's turn in an alarm and get the hell away from here!"

They turned in the alarm and walked casually away from the burning building. Tork called for the pick-up. The van arrived and forty minutes later they were back in Manhattan.

After they parted, Jake went back to his apartment. He felt good about what he had just done. He had just set fire to a warehouse and destroyed the contraband weapons that some nefarious organization, a band of terrorist geeks, was going to use to harm the people of the United States and compromise the security of the nation. Jake Barrada smiled with satisfaction because he believed that he actually accomplished something good—something that had real meaning and importance.

That feeling was reinforced when Phil Niekrom called him on Tuesday to say that *Operation Silk Worm* was a success. The FBI had the evidence it needed to move in on Tabor Import & Export and close the whole operation down. When he heard that, Jake felt an added measure of pride, because he knew that he had contributed to that success and he was sure that he had latched on to the career field that he was born to follow.

CHAPTER 5

After *Operation Silk Worm*, Jake went out as an apprentice on a second assignment. This time he assisted Chuck, another experienced field agent. Together they penetrated an office in a large building in Newark. They entered the office after midnight and planted miniature surveillance cameras and listening devices in the nooks and crannies of the office. The code name for that mission was *Operation Eye-Spy*. Jake never received any feedback as to whether their efforts were successful or not so he assumed that it was an on-going operation and maybe he would get a progress report at a later time.

Two months later, Jake got another assignment. This time he assisted an agent named Wolf. The two men went to an office complex in Long Island. The plan was simple enough, all they had to do was break into the main office, open files and search for evidence of terrorist activity. They photographed anything incriminating or suspicious then they put everything back in order, left the premises, and faded into the night.

After three field assignments as an apprentice, Jake was given a solo mission. It was similar to *Operation Eye-Spy* but in a different location. He was sent to break into an office and plant miniature surveillance cameras and listening devices in hidden niches and recesses. He was a little nervous about going out on mission by himself without anyone to guide him and watch his back, but he knew that this was a step that he would eventually have to take so he gamely accepted the assignment. As it turned out, everything went off without a hitch. Completing a successful mission as a solo operative gave Jake a feeling of accomplishment and instilled the self-confidence in him that gave him the courage to tackle another mission on his own.

That opportunity came the following month. This assignment was like the previous ones but this time he ran into an unexpected predicament. He was working well after midnight in the office of a large international shipping firm. He had just searched the office files and taken photographs of a number of papers, records and documents that he thought should be passed on to the federal authorities. He was closing all the files and arranging everything the way he found it, when the sudden call of nature gave him the uneasy feeling that his full bladder was about to burst. He was faced with the urgent need to relieve himself but was faced with the problem of *where to go?* He looked around hoping to see a toilet in the office but to his dismay there were no adjacent facilities.

He then assumed that the restrooms must be in the hall. Jake closed all the files and put everything back in order as quickly as he could. He knew that time was of the essence and he tried to move as swiftly and expeditiously as possible before his muscles gave way to a biological accident. After returning everything to its original condition, Jake stepped out into the hall and closed and locked the office door behind him.

He looked down the hall and saw the restroom door. He hurried to it, anticipating that relief was only minutes away. Then again, maybe not. When he tried to open the door, Jake found to his chagrin that it was locked. *Strategic Planning* hadn't foreseen this contingency and *Reconnaissance* hadn't provided a key to the restroom door. Jake stood outside the locked door thwarted as to what to do next. Operational agents are instructed not to leave any trace of their activity on a covert mission, but how does one avoid leaving a puddle of pee when nature demands relief?

As his internal pressures mounted, threatening a loss of self-control, Jake spotted a potted palm at the end of the hall. He rushed to it. He stood before the pot, unzipped his fly, extracted his personal watering hose and released a stream of bodily fluid into the soil surrounding the trunk of the palm tree. Jake breathed a sigh of relief as he felt his internal pressures abate. At the same time, he looked down and hoped that the soil in the pot could absorb and contain all the liquid that he was pumping into it. It did. When Jake finished he tucked his organ away and composed himself, then he left the building to disappear into the surrounding metropolis.

When he returned to his apartment, Jake kicked off his sneakers, plopped down into a nearby chair and reviewed all that he had done that night. He felt that he had accomplished his mission, but at the same time he recognized that there was a curious twist to this night's venture: in addition to ferreting out suspicious documents and files he was unexpectedly caught off guard by the urgent need to take a whiz. This was something that *Strategic Planning* with all its meticulous, careful and precise attention to detail had not anticipated. And Jake came to understand that every time he tackled a mission he might encounter the unexpected and the unforeseen and it would be up to him to peel his own banana.

There were no field assignments for the next three months. Jake was beginning to get bored with only his personal training business to keep him occupied. The days dragged on and Jake was beginning to wonder if he would ever get another assignment. He speculated that maybe word somehow got out about him urinating in the potted palm and perhaps the honchos at BRIA decided that he had violated the protocol by leaving a trace of his presence behind and maybe they decided that Jake was no longer a trustworthy agent. Although, as he thought about it, Jake couldn't see how anyone could know about his pee since it was absorbed by the moist soil in some mute potted palm at the end of the hallway.

The days went by, then Jake received an email saying that there was a job to be done and he should report to the *warehouse* on the Westside the following Monday. He would be assigned to work with operations supervisor, Max Beltrane. When he read that message, Jake was elated because he had another mission to go out on.

On Monday morning, Jake Barrada emerged from the subterranean subway station to street level and walked West to the black, grimy building with the sign *United Warehouse Facilities*. He approached the front door, looked up and down the street to be sure that there was no one about then he punched the number sequence on the digital-combination lock and opened the door. He entered the dingy foyer and went immediately to the fetid stairwell and he vaulted up the steps to the first-floor security entrance. He executed the secret access ritual and was admitted to the undercover world of BRIA headquarters.

Once inside, Jake paused to look around and acclimate himself to the activity about him. Even though he had been here many times before, he was still alert to anything new or different. His field experience had conditioned him to be alert and mindful of his surroundings at all times. He stood there motionless for a few minutes, observing, scrutinizing, studying every detail of the office complex. He watched the people as they moved about and interacted with each other and formed a mental picture of what each person was doing.

When he was satisfied that he had absorbed everything, Jake walked down a long hallway looking for the office of Max Beltrane. Along the way he ran into Phil Niekrom.

They exchanged brief greetings, then Phil asked, "morning Jake. What brings you here? Got another assignment?"

"Yeah, but I don't know what it is yet. I just got the call yesterday and I imagine that I'll find out what it's all about soon."

"Who's the *Operations Supervisor*?" asked Niekrom.

"A guy by the name of Max Beltrane. The name is familiar but I can't place the face."

"Hmmm, Beltrane you say. I think that he's new to operations, but if I'm not mistaken his office is three doors down the hall."

Jake thanked Niekrom then walked down the hall to find Beltrane's office. The door was open; a man was seated at his desk absorbed in his computer screen. Jake knocked on the door frame.

"Max Beltrane?" he asked. The man nodded. "I'm Jake Barrada. I got a message from you saying that we've got a mission and that I'm on your team. What's up?"

At the sound of Jake's voice, Max turned from the screen and stood up. His expression changed from somber-serious to all smiles and sunny disposition. He extended his hand across the desk.

"Jake Barrada! You are a sight for sore eyes. When I saw your name, I remembered that we once worked together in *Information Acquisitions*.

How long has it been since we last worked together? Too long, much too long! Well, no matter because we're going to work together again."

Jake was taken aback by Max's over-the-top enthusiasm. Jake vaguely remembered that he and Max had worked together in *Information Acquisitions* but that was over a year ago and their working relationship was brief and of no importance. As he studied Max, Jake recollected the assignment that two of them had worked together on. It was a routine research and data-analysis project—basically desk work that amounted to little more than arranging statistical data and organizing random facts and reports. That project was done in the office building on Sixth Avenue and their assignment lasted less than a month. After that, Jake never gave it a second thought but it seemed that Max Beltrane had a vivid memory of their work together. Moreover, it seemed that he had an over-inflated opinion of their working relationship and Jake was unprepared for Max's spontaneous fervor and spirited saccharine personality.

It seemed, however, that Max was just getting started and he continued. "Yes indeed, I feel that this will be an auspicious moment when we rekindle our working partnership. It will be like old times only this time it will be a little different because we're going out on a field assignment together. We will get to work together hand-in-glove to tackle an actual assignment away from the office environment. We'll be going into enemy territory to grab the bull by the horns and beard the lion in his den. I believe that this entire adventure will be stimulating and exciting and I can't wait to get started. Come in and have a seat and I'll tell you all about it."

Jake walked in, wondering if he was about to get caught up in a whirlwind of enthusiastic rapture and a barrage of mixed metaphors. He seated himself and looked at Max as he came around from behind the desk. Max was average height and chubby. He was wearing light-beige chino slacks, a white shirt and red tie. To Jake he looked more like a high-school history teacher than the bureaucrat-agent that he was. His official title was *Operations Supervisor* which was a vague appellation that was created to suggest a mundane administrative position without actually giving any significant clue as to the specific nature of the job.

That was a typical ploy of BRIA—just give enough information to establish your position without revealing exactly what you do.

As Jake was seated the picture of the brief working relationship that he had with Max and of his ebullient personality came into focus and it made Jake wonder to himself how Max was able to secure a position as an *Operations Supervisor* in BRIA. That seemed odd to Jake because he remembered Max as having an overly effervescent personality that was in contrast to the rest of the people who worked in *Operations*.

In *Operations*, all the employees maintain an intense, focused demeanor in the work environment as they concentrate with almost hypnotic intensity on their objectives. They are keenly aware that loose, non-judicial talk could jeopardize the security of their organization; so, they limit their conversations to serious, terse dialogue that is relevant to the current mission. No one talks about their personal lives or asks questions about what the other employees do outside the office.

These people are the norm, but Max Beltrane seemed to be somewhat of an anomaly. Based on their brief experience working together, Jake believed that Max was a hard worker always dedicated to the task he was engaged in, but still his personality seemed to be at odds with others in the company. While everyone else was taciturn and subdued, Max appeared to be verbose, loquacious and animated. Jake felt that Max behaved more like a combination of a motivational speaker and a television game-show host than the stereotypical operative in the tight-lipped BRIA organization.

Jake remembered that there were even times when Max's hyper energy seemed boundless. He was a live wire in the Spartan environment of laconic, closed-mouthed hoplites. Jake often thought that Max was like a verbal volcano, sometimes dormant, but ready to erupt at any moment with burst of hot air and a barrage of words. Sometimes, the slightest verbal clue would launch Max off into a tangential thought pattern that would start him rhapsodizing on any subject that was only vaguely connected to the matter at hand.

Nevertheless, Jake knew that in spite of all his exuberant outbursts, Max maintained his discipline; he never disclosed confidential information, compromised objectives or talked about himself or inquired about others. Jake noticed that there were even a few times when Max was subdued, when he discarded his verbosity and came directly to the point; but these seemed to be rare occurrences that made Jake wonder if there was an underlying reason for them or if Max simply ran out of wind and energy.

All of this didn't matter as long Max worked in an office handling papers and shifting data, but Jake wondered how Max would behave on a field assignment—whether he could sharpen his focus and tame his tongue or whether his boundless exuberance would get the better of him. *And if so, what would be the consequences of all that zeal?* Well, this time they would be going out together, and Jake suspected that he would soon learn the answer to that question.

"Well, well, Jake I'm glad you're here," spouted Max with overflowing energy. "You have any trouble getting here? I mean, were the subways all running on time? Didn't have to push your way through throngs of pedestrians, fight against the tide of oncoming human cattle, maneuver among the zombie commuters? Struggle against the vicissitudes of nature? Get caught up in the tides of human collective motion?"

"No Max, everything was fine. Tell me," asked Jake suspiciously, "how many field missions have you worked?"

"Well Jake, to be honest with you, this is my first assignment as an *Operations Supervisor.*" Max noticed Jake's wary look and quickly added, "Not to worry Jake, I assisted other supervisors on other missions and I am positive that I have learned the ropes and mastered the complexities of field operations. You are looking at a pillar of self-confidence, a paragon of efficiency, a model of competence. A man who is ready to take charge and pilot our mission to a successful conclusion."

"Whatever you say, Max." said Jake, unimpressed by Max's bravado. "Now, suppose we talk about—"

"Yes, Jake," said Max, cutting off Jake before he could finish his thought. "I must say that I am proud and excited to be here, because I feel that I am part of a noble organization that is working toward a grandiose objective. I feel that I am a part of a patriotic endeavor that will keep our great country safe and secure."

Jake listened to Max's ostentatious discourse without saying a word but at the same time, he wondered when it would all come to an end.

"Yes indeed! Every time I come to work here and I look at the grungy outside of this building and I see the big picture underlying it. I see the subtle design behind the image that the masterminds at BRIA have created so that the company can remain innocuous and unobtrusive. I understand that by creating this grungy, seemingly poorly-maintained edifice with an unsightly exterior, BRIA is able to house this entire, high-tech, secret operation in the heart of Manhattan without anyone suspecting that it is really here. The broken elevator, black grimy facade, the dingy exterior, the rust and graffiti, the lifeless appearance, the desolate location, the dilapidated interior; that's all camouflage to keep our presence hidden from prying eyes of curious, nosy, inquisitive people.

"You see how clever that is? You have to admit, Jake, that this is pure genius, real method within the madness, a masterpiece of covert design! Every morning when I come to work and look up at the facade I have to admire the ingenuity behind the decrepit image. Why it's almost as if they called up the spirit and genius of Leonardo DaVinci to mastermind the effect. Why, there is more than just science behind the disguise, there is also art. And most important, we are part of that grand design. We are a part of a grand organization that is safe-guarding American democracy."

"Yeah, yeah!" said Jake. "Whatever you say. Can you come down out of the clouds and get to the assignment, the reason that you summoned me here?"

"Ah, yes of course, Jake. The assignment, our current objective, our *raison d'etre*; that's what we want to talk about. That's what I like about you Jake. You get right to the point; no beating around the bush. No small talk. A man of action, that's what you are. Always prepared, always ready to get into the thick of things, ever ready to face the challenges and demands encountered in the complex world of espionage."

Jake rolled his eyes at Max's motor-mouthed prolix. *Was there no end to this man's prattle?*

"Enough Max! What's our objective? Tell me about the assignment!"

"The assignment. Yes, we should talk about that. Right now, without losing time. Our research team, technicians and strategic planners have put together a set-up that I think will interest and excite you. And if I do say so myself, these guys have really outdone themselves in devising the perfect plan. Follow me and prepare to be amazed."

CHAPTER 6

Max walked out of his office with Jake following close behind. They walked down the hall and took an interior elevator, which was in good working order, to the fifth floor. On the fifth floor they entered a room. In the center of the room there was a table with a scale model of a building on it. Max stepped aside and allowed Jake to approach the model. Jake walked around the table studying the Lilliputian building from every angle. He was taken with how perfect the little structure was. It seemed like the model makers had captured every detail of the building and rendered the bricks, windows, doors, and all the structural nuances in perfect miniature. In addition to the building model, there were landscaping features, miniature trees, bushes, and rocks all there to show the model building in its natural surroundings.

Jake looked up at Max and asked, "Where is this building? I mean the real thing, the building that this model was made from."

"It's Upstate, a little over two hours' drive from here?"

"What's in it? I mean what is its function?"

Max grimaced. "We can only guess. We think that it houses a bunch of electronic surveillance hardware that intercepts satellite transmissions, hacks into web sites, taps data banks and gathers all information in any way it can. We don't know who is at the controls, who pushes the buttons, or pulls the strings or why they are doing this or what they are planning."

"Can't we hack into their system? Surely we have the brains in this organization to get into the cyber-backdoor of this place."

"We have the brains and they did try hacking into the system, but the geeks inside have set up air gaps between their internet connection, the data collection, and transmission system. So far, we haven't been able to bridge that gap."

"And we have no idea what they're planning, their purpose, the reason behind all the activities?" asked Jake.

"We think that they may be preparing for some sort of cyber-attack. We are also sure they are not working alone, because they transmit all the intelligence that they gather."

"Transmit?! "Transmit to who?"

"To whom, Jake. Object of the preposition. To whom."

"Okay Mr. grammarian. I stand corrected. To whom are these geeks transmitting the intelligence?"

"We don't know that either. We tried intercepting the transmissions coming out, but no soap. The transmissions that we were able to capture were all encoded and jumbled. We got nothing. And we had no way of finding out who was receiving them."

"Okay, so what about this end; the building itself? Who works there? Who owns it? There must be some paperwork somewhere showing registration and occupancy."

Max shook his head. "No! Another dead end. We tried tracing the ownership of the building but found that it was a large dummy corporation, part of a humongous holding company. We tried investigating the corporation from every possible angle but no dice. We came to roadblocks at every turn. On the surface, everything seems to be on the up and up, but we suspect otherwise. Unfortunately, we have no definite proof, nothing really solid, only suspicions."

"Suspicions of what? What stinks?" asked Jake. "If everything seems on the level, what is it that got your hackles up?"

"Hackles! That's cute Jake. I like the way you throw in these nifty, little words here and there. They're little verbal surprises, choice bon mots that add color to your speech. I find it stimulating talking to you Jake; because you display such variety in your expressions, such originality in your phraseology."

Jake rolled his eyes. Max was off on another one of his florid, verbal tangents. No use interrupting him. The only thing to do was let him run his train of thought until he ran out of hot air. Presently he did just that and said, "Now, where were we?"

"You were about to tell me why you think the building is dirty and what you think might be going on inside."

"Yeah! That's what I was getting to. We've been watching this building for some time now. We have satellite surveillance from above and we have hidden agents in the surrounding woods night and day, twenty-four seven. After studying all the reports, we noticed some curious details."

"Like what, exactly?"

"Well, let's start with the perimeter fence that encircles the building. It's a chain-link fence, eight-feet high. The top is laced with coils of razor ribbon. Why the exaggerated security if the building is on the up-and-up? But there's more. The fence is wired."

"You mean electrified."

"No, not quite. We think the fence is wired with sensors. Anyone or anything that touches the fence sets off an alarm inside. We found this out when one of our hidden agents from *Surveillance* was working in the woods at night. He saw a raccoon brush up against the fence. In less than a minute security guards came rushing out to see what was on the fence. It appears that the raccoon set off an alarm inside just by touching the fence, but otherwise the critter was unharmed and went on its merry way."

"Yeah, sensors. That sound's plausible."

"There may be sensors on the building itself, but we're not certain. And then there is the area between the fence and the building."

Jake looked at the model. "I don't see anything."

"No, it's not on the model. Step over to the screen and I'll show you."

Max walked over to a large screen on the wall. The screen was blank, but at the touch of a button the screen lit up and a picture appeared.

"This is a picture taken from a satellite. You can't see anything at this distance, but I'll bring up the magnification. Watch!" Max punched a button again and again. As the magnification increased, the image of the building came into view, but the details were still vague. A few more punches of the button and everything became clear. "There Jake, now you can see what's between the fence and the building."

Jake saw what was not on the model. "Dogs!"

"Yes, Jake, guard dogs. From four to six guard dogs roaming around the building at any one time. Day and night. Twenty-four, seven. And from all appearances they look vicious."

Jake thought about this. "Hmmm, vicious guard dogs, encrypted transmissions, and an ultra-high security fence wired with sensors. I admit it does sound suspicious. You got anything else?"

"Yes, something. There have been times when our on-ground surveillance agents recorded some curious characters going in and out of the building. We traced these guys. None of them were notorious in themselves, but they appear shady because we followed them and found that they sometimes contacted agents and operatives of known terrorist organizations."

"Okay, assuming that the place is a den of iniquity, what do we do now? Jam their transmissions? Shut the whole operation down? Poison the dogs? What?"

"Den of iniquity! Jake you are a storehouse of colorful expressions. Poison the dogs? You have a vivid imagination! That's why I like—"

"Enough Max!" interrupted Jake, clearly annoyed that Max was about to launch into one of his many verbose meanderings. "Get to the objective. What are we going to do? Have we got a plan?"

"Yes, Jake we have a plan; we have given it the code name, *Operation Dense Fog*, and it doesn't involve shutting the place down or poisoning any dogs. Quite the opposite in fact. Our plan is to send a man inside and have him secretly plant a couple of tandem electronic gadgets within the circuitry of their computer-transmission system. After he plants the bugs he gets out without leaving a trace.

"Our specialized devices will be hidden inside the circuitry, where they will latch onto their software and seek out vulnerabilities in their code. They'll copy whatever information the geeks gather and send it to our receivers before it can be encoded. We will have an inside ear to what is being gathered and sent out. We may even be able to find out who's behind their operation and get a glimpse of their objectives. Is that not diabolically clever or what?"

"I take it that I am the man selected to go inside and plant the specialized devices."

"Bravo Jake! Yes indeed, we believe that you are the ideal man to carry out this assignment. You are a man of rare talent and proven ability. A man, battle-tested, and resourceful in the face of adversity, a modern swashbuckler in the tradition of Douglas Fairbanks, Errol Flynn, Indiana Jones—"

"Can the corny praise and vintage movie trivia, Max! Save it for my eulogy. I have two questions."

"Shoot!"

"Question one: assuming that I can get inside this fortress, how will I know where to find the transmission system and once I find it, how will I know exactly where to plant our gizmos in the circuitry?"

"Good question. We have a pretty good idea as to the layout inside the building. We were able to get a peek inside a couple of months ago. As it happened, the air conditioning system in the place started to malfunction. The geeks inside called a local HVAC company to come and fix it. We were able to attach a couple of our guys from *Reconnaissance* to the maintenance team. The team stretched out the maintenance for a couple of weeks, during which time our guys were able to sneak around, get a feel for the general layout of the inside and they even managed to surreptitiously take a few pictures with a hidden camera. So, we are pretty confident that we know the inside layout."

"What about the transmitter itself?" asked Jake. "How sure are you that you know the circuitry?"

"Pretty sure. One of our guys managed to get into the transmitter room. He made the excuse that air conditioning is vital to keep electronic machines from overheating. The geeks bought it and he got in. While he was faking a maintenance task, he was able to take pictures with his hidden camera. Our experts studied the photos and were able to determine the type of transmitter in the place. It wasn't difficult; most transmitters have similar designs and components. What's your second question?"

"How the hell do I get inside?"

"Ah yes, the sixty-four, thousand-dollar question. I'll answer that question, but first I'll let you ponder the problem and chew on it for a bit. Study the model before you and the image on the screen. How would you get inside? Use your imagination, consider the variables, evaluate the options and see what you can come up with on the spur of the moment, off the top of your head."

Jake turned from Max and focused on the building model. Then he studied the satellite picture on the wall screen. He looked from one to the other and back again. He considered all the obstacles and he conjured up mental scenarios to get over or around them. He imagined that he could get over the fence with a light-weight, portable ladder. He had practiced with them and even used one on a field assignment. He found that they were collapsible, easy to carry and quick to set up. But as he looked at the model saw that he would have to brace the ladder against the fence and that would set off the sensor alarms wired into the fence. Not good.

Even if he did get over the fence there would be the dogs to contend with. He would have to put them out of commission and quickly. Jake was aware that there were knock-out sprays that he could use to incapacitate the dogs, but he would have to get all of the dogs quickly. If he missed even one animal it would be on him in a flash and tear him to pieces. Six dogs in less than a minute. Next to impossible.

Maybe there was another way. If he climbed one of the trees outside the fence, he might be able to shoot a line to the roof. That way he could ride the line over the fence and dogs and get straight to the building. *Yes, but how would he anchor the line to the roof? And if he could get onto the roof would there be sensors that he would have to contend with?* Maybe, maybe not. Assuming that he could get that far he would have to face the next problem: *how would he get inside the place?*

All of these plans had possibilities and given time, he might be able to work out the snags, but each had the same obvious flaw; they all left a trace of an outsider. They announced that an intruder had penetrated the building and left evidence that the security had been compromised. That would defeat the whole purpose of this assignment. The objective was to get inside the building, plant the tandem bugs and make a clean getaway without anyone knowing that a perpetrator had ever been there. The more he thought about it, the more he realized that this was definitely a thorny problem and there didn't seem to be any solution to it. Maybe there was a way, but if so, Jake couldn't see it.

At this moment Jake became aware that Max was completely silent. He hadn't said a word during the last five minutes. This was totally uncharacteristic of Max.

Jake turned his attention from the model to Max.

"Why are you so quite all of a sudden? What's the matter? Cat got your tongue?"

"I'm watching you Jake. It's fascinating watching you as you study and scrutinize the model and the screen. I can almost see your mind working, calculating, analyzing; absorbing every detail, taking in all the angles, considering the objective, evaluating all the pitfalls, pondering the possibilities. Watching you is like watching a well-tuned, mental machine working. Wheels turning, relays clicking, circuits lighting up, running mental algorithms, devising plans, formulating schemes. It is like melody and symphony coming together to produce analyzed, coherent cogitation."

"Spare me your poetic descriptions, Shakespeare. I give up. It seems impossible, but I'm sure that the brains in *Strategic Planning* have already solved the problem. So, tell me how we crack this nut. Out with it. How do I get inside the fortress?"

"Simple, Jake; you fly in."

"Fly in?" asked Jake skeptically. "In what? A chopper?"

"No, Jake, a chopper's too big. It makes too much noise."

"A hang glider."

"Nope. A hang glider is still too big. What's more it's too hard to maneuver precisely from point to point. A sudden, unexpected gust of wind could throw you off target. You might end up in the dog pit. We wouldn't want that."

"No, we wouldn't want that," Jake echoed sarcastically. "No chopper, no hang glider. What else is there?"

"Oh Jake," said Max with mock disappointment, "I'm surprised at you. You are ignoring the obvious. You fly in on a drone."

"A drone is an unmanned flying vehicle."

"That's right Jake. This drone will be guided to the objective by a technician stationed at the jumping-off point. You'll be riding as a passenger not as the pilot."

"A drone might just do it. They are quiet, but it would have to be big enough to carry me, yet small enough to land on the roof without anyone spotting it coming in or setting off any roof sensors. Can we get one like that? "

"Yes, Jake. We already have one. Would you like to see it?"

Jake nodded and Max led him into an adjoining room. In the center of this room was a platform with a small drone resting on it. Jake approached the platform and looked incredulously at the drone.

"This?! You expect me to ride on this! This is just a toy. It doesn't look like the wing span is even thirty-six inches."

"Thirty-four inches."

"What's its range?"

"About ten miles."

"And what is the load capacity?"

"Five pounds."

"What? Oh, come off it, Max. You can't be serious. I weigh over a hundred and ninety-five pounds. If I sat on this thing I'd smash it."

"I am serious, Jake. And you're right, you would smash it if you sat on it the way you are now. But you won't be the way you are now."

Jake looked warily at Max. Max was quiet, but he had a subtle smile on his puss. Jake could tell that Max had a surprise up his sleeve and was waiting to spring the punch line.

"What do you mean that I won't be the way that I am now. How will I be different?"

"Turn around and look behind you," replied Max. "The answer to your question is right there."

CHAPTER 7

Jake turned around and saw a huge machine. He didn't pay any attention to it when he walked into the room because he was focused on the drone, but now it captured his full attention. The machine ran the length of the entire wall. It had lights, knobs, switches, buttons, dials, and assorted electronic indicators. It resembled a mainframe computer, but there was one significant difference; in the center of the machine was a glass door, much like a shower door.

"What is it?" asked Jake. "What does this monstrosity do?"

"It's a reducing machine Jake. It was developed by *Research and Development*. They have been putting it together for more than a year. R & D said that this machine takes all sorts of things, even living beings, and makes them smaller. When *Strategic Planning* heard about it, they figured that it might just be the ideal thing to penetrate *Dense Fog*."

Jake looked back at Max. "*R & D* said it makes things smaller. How do they know that? Have they tested this thing?"

"Yes, they have," replied Max. "You have to understand that I was not in on this from the beginning, so I am only telling you what I was told. As I understand it, *R & D* knew that they were dealing with radically new technology and at that time they couldn't be certain what the results would be; so, they were very careful with their experiments. They started out by trying to shrink inanimate objects, books, staplers, cell phones, rolls of toilet paper, anything that they had around, just to see what would work and what wouldn't. Then they became more systematic in their tests. They chose their materials carefully, kept exact records and made a detailed analysis of each material as they tested it. After a lot of testing and trial and error, they developed a catalog of hundreds of materials that can be made smaller."

"How much smaller?"

"Well, as I understand it, they haven't tested its full potential, but they claim it can reduce a full-grown man to six inches."

"Six inches!" cried Jake. "Have they actually tried it on a human being?"

"Yes, but not at first. After testing hundreds of materials, they went to the next step. They went to experimenting on organic things like fruits, vegetables, meat, and plants. They wanted to see how living materials reacted to the process. According to the reports, the machine worked like a dream and the results were truly amazing. It made these items small enough so they could fit in a doll's house.

"At that point, *R & D* figured that they were ready to try to shrink living, breathing creatures. They started with animals. Rabbits at first, then cats. Then they went to dogs and even put a chimpanzee in the machine. As far as they could tell there didn't seem to be any ill effects, but of course, none of these creatures could talk so the experimenters really couldn't be sure if the subjects felt anything out of the ordinary. But the results were encouraging, so they figured that it was time to take the next step, the giant step, the big leap, and test a human being in the machine.

"Some time during all this testing, *Strategic Planning* got wind of this machine; they figured that it showed real potential for field operations and they wanted to get involved. That's when I came on board and became part of the team. I got to be there about the time when *R & D* was ready to run human trials. Since there was some potential risk involved, they asked for volunteers. A guy from data analysis stepped up to the plate. Tom Jenkins, maybe you know him?"

Jake shook his head.

"Yeah, Tom Jenkins, a real nice guy. You should get to know him. Anyway, Tommy, our intrepid volunteer, stepped into the machine and an *R & D* technician turned on the juice."

"And...?"

"The machine shrunk him Jake," cried Max with obvious delight. "It took Tom Jenkins, all five-foot, eleven inches of him, and reduced him to six inches."

"How did he feel after that? Any ill effects?"

Max shook his head. "No Jake, he said that he didn't feel a thing. It was curious though. He said that it didn't seem like he was shrinking, but it was more like the world was growing larger all around him. It boggles the mind. Can you possibly imagine what it must be like to see the world getting bigger and growing all around you? That must be an amazing thrill, to see everything around you growing like plants and objects on steroids.

"Well, when *R & D* was certain that Jenkins was all right, they asked for more volunteers. And six people came forward. They stepped into the machine—not all together, but one at a time. It shrunk them, each of them. It worked like a charm. If I wasn't there to see it, I wouldn't have believed it."

Jake looked back at the humongous machine. "How does this thing work? How is it able to shrink living things without harming them?"

"Well," said Max, "I'll try to explain how it works, in theory at least. You have to understand that my explanation will only be superficial without all the technical details or specifics. I can only relate what was told to me by the *R & D* experts, because, after all, as you know Jake, I only came into this at a late stage, and I am not a scientist, and physics and microbiology are not my fields of expertise. It's not that I'm stupid or anything like that, it's just that I haven't really had the time to study those fields in depth. At the same time, I am not a complete neophyte. I have done some reading and self-study so I do understand the basic concepts of modern science."

"All right Max, enough with the disclaimers! I get it that you are not Einstein and you're not Dopey. Just tell me what you do know about the machine."

"Okay, as you know everything in the universe is made up of atoms. I'm sure that you are aware of the basic structure of the atom. An atom is made up of a nucleus and electrons. The nucleus is made up of protons and neutrons. There are other subatomic particles of course, but we can ignore them for our purposes."

Thank God! thought Jake to himself as he stood there trying to be patient with Max's exaggerated and seemingly endless, verbal contortions.

"So," continued Max, "we have the nucleus and the electrons. But they are not together. In fact, electro-magnetic forces keep them far apart. Now this distance may not seem like much to us because we are talking about the teeny-weeny, tiny, ity-bity world of the atom, a world we cannot see but only imagine. But if we could get inside the atom, we would see that this distance is immense.

"Now, I am told that if a nucleus was to be enlarged to the size of a baseball and placed on the pitcher's mound of a major league stadium, the electron would be somewhere out in the bleachers. Can you picture that Jake? On an atomic level we are talking about vast distances. Think about that Jake. That means that within each of us there are billions and billions of protons and electrons and miles and miles of vast empty space. One of the technicians told me ninety-nine percent of an atom is an empty void.

"That means that ninety-nine percent of you and me is empty space. Makes you stop and think, doesn't it Jake? Makes you wonder about the majesty and complexity of the universe. It's a humbling thought to know that each of us is but a small cog in the immense machinery of the vast, complex cosmos, and that most of everything everywhere is nothing, but a vast empty void. Isn't that positively amazing?"

"Yeah, right," said Jake dryly, "I'm bowled over with awe; now can we get to the part where you tell me how the machine works."

"Yes, that's right; the machine," said Max, "I was coming to that. Well, this machine doesn't change the basic atomic particles. What is does do, is mitigate the atomic, electromagnetic forces between the nucleus and electrons so that the space between them is diminished and they come closer and closer together. In effect, it makes the atom smaller without really changing the atomic particles. That is how the machine can reduce objects, animals, and people."

"What about these people you reduced?" asked Jake. "Are they still running around like little chipmunks?"

"Little chipmunks! That's cute Jake. It reminds me of a Disney cartoon. Now who were the Disney chipmunks again? Ah yes, Chip and Dale. Amusing little creatures. I think there's a new movie out about them. But no matter, to answer your question, no, they have all returned to their normal size."

"This machine do that?" asked Jake.

"It didn't have to. The restoration process happens naturally. The electro-magnetic forces inside the atom eventually reassert themselves and the machine's effect wears off. When that happens, the electrons and protons will move apart to assume their natural distance and the subject automatically grows back to normal size. All our volunteers have returned to their original shapes and sizes without using the machine. And they came back without any ill effects, no complaints, no abnormalities. That's because the process is scale invariant."

"What does that mean?" asked Jake.

"Scale invariant? I'm glad you asked that Jake, because I didn't know that either. Not at first, but then I asked questions and I listened and learned. Now I can say that I'm—"

"Max, just tell me what scale invariant means!"

"Okay Jake. I was getting around to that. It means that the reducing process didn't change the normal body functions of the subjects when they changed size."

"How long did it take the miniature subjects to grow back to normal size?"

"Well, they stayed small for about an hour then they just started to sprout up. It just happened. It was like nature taking over again. As some nameless pundit aptly put it, 'Nature always comes to bat last!'

"That was the way it was for most of the subjects, but there were a couple of variations. It took one guy about an hour and fifteen minutes before he started to grow, but he was big and kinda fat. We figure that he had more atoms than the other people so it took him longer to come around. He was more like an exception. Although *R & D* noticed another factor besides size and weight could affect the growth process."

"Which is…?" asked Jake.

"Metabolic rate. One of our subjects, a young, athletic woman started doing exercises while she was tiny. She took a piece of string and started jumping rope. You should have seen her Jake. This little figure of a woman jumping rope. It was cute, but totally unreal. Anyway, after about thirty minutes of jumping she sat down to rest. That's when she started to grow, not to her full size, but only to about twelve inches tall. Then she stopped and remained at twelve inches for about twenty minutes. After that, she started growing again, this time to her full size."

"Are you sure the guys in *R & D* have worked out all the bugs in this system?" asked Jake skeptically. "Sounds like they're still a bit fuzzy about a lot of the details and it seems like there's still much to learn. Wouldn't it be better to take the time to run additional experiments, evaluate the results, and get more precise data?"

"Jake, you are forgetting the mission. Consider our objective. What we have here in this building is a possible den of iniquity, to use your expression. We have no idea what is going on inside this place. We suspect that this building may be a stronghold for closet spies and undercover terrorists. We don't know their plans are or how far they are into them. For all we know they could be planning something extreme, possibly in the very near future. Time may be of the essence. We feel that it is imperative that we get into the building as soon as possible and plant our bugs so we can get a handle on their operations before these geeks get their act together and do something drastic."

"Point taken," replied Jake. "Okay, I see what we have to work with. Let me go over everything that you told me to see if I understand how we're going to execute this operation."

"Go ahead Jake! Pick up the ball and run with it. Engage your brain, harness your cognitive machine and put all the pieces together to come up with a complete picture of the operation. Set your mighty intellect to work, see if you can come up with a workable plan. I'll let you concentrate without any interference from me. I'll just sit here on the edge of my seat, fully attentive, watching as you evaluate the details and assemble them into a foolproof strategy. I won't say a word; I'll let you do your thing."

Max fell silent, ready, waiting to see if Jake could put all the pieces together and come up with a workable, coherent plan. He assumed the posture of a passive listener, giving Jake his full, undivided attention; but there was a faint smile on his face because he knew something that Jake didn't know. There was one piece of information missing from the setup. There was one detail, an important link, that he hadn't revealed to Jake, and without that one bit of information there was no way that Jake could create a perfect workable plan. Max waited with silent anticipation, intently watching Jake to see if he would discover the hidden glitch and catch the subtle flaw.

Jake began, "Okay, let me see if I've got this. I step into this miraculous machine and it shrinks me to doll size. Small enough to climb onto the drone; but this drone has a limited range of only ten miles, so we have to drive to somewhere Upstate to get a takeoff point within a ten-mile radius of the building. At that point I mount the drone and a technician will guide it to the rooftop of our target building."

After saying that, Jake paused to ponder the situation. Max was watching Jake as he mentally considered all the elements and tried to work them into his plan. When Jake paused, Max suspected that Jake had stumbled onto the flaw, the missing piece, the one important detail in the set-up that hadn't been revealed. Max waited to hear what Jake would say.

"Wait a minute Max, there's something wrong here."

"What Jake?" asked Max with feigned surprise, "What's wrong?"

"There's something about this set-up that doesn't click. You told me that the drone has a limited range of ten miles. That means that the launch point will have to be close to the target. Now the target, the building, is somewhere Upstate. You said that if we drive, it will take us a little over two hours to get there. Am I right so far?"

"Right on!" said Max with a gleam in his eye. He was enjoying watching and listening as Jake was coming to the delicious moment when he pounced on the glitch in the plan.

"So, here's the part that doesn't add up; if I step into this machine and it reduces me to chipmunk size, then we get into a vehicle and start driving Upstate. I'll start growing after about an hour. I'll be fully grown—back to my normal size—before we get half-way to the target. I'll be too big to sit in this baby aircraft. On the other hand, we can't launch the drone from here because the target is beyond the ten-mile flight range of the drone. Even if we could send the drone with me on it from here, flying time would be over an hour. Either way, you can't reduce me and get me within ten miles of the target building before I grow back to my full size."

"Bravo, Jake! You put the pieces together, successfully analyzed the situation, and discovered the hidden stumbling block, the subtle flaw, the missing link, the fly in the ointment, the itch you could not scratch. I knew that with your keen analytic mind, sagacious intellect, and sharp perception you would evaluate all the information, dissect the strategy and spot the snag. I was sure that you would do it, and you didn't disappoint me. I'm proud of you."

"Stop it Max! You're playing games. There's something you haven't told me. What is it that I'm missing?"

"You're right Jake, there is something more. Something I didn't tell you earlier because I didn't want to overload you with too much information. Now you're for the missing piece to the puzzle. The key to unlock the conundrum. Here it is; this machine has another component. It's not as big as this one and it's not a complete machine. It's not here. We installed it in our mobile command post, a Winnebago. It's downstairs in the garage and ready to go. It's kinda like an extension unit and it works in conjunction with this one here, but we can operate it from a remote location. And with this unit we can get close enough to Dense Fog to launch the whole operation!"

CHAPTER 8

Max warmed up to his subject with obvious delight and launched into the full explanation.

"Now, here's the complete plan. You step into this machine here; we'll call it the mother machine as opposed to the remote unit in the Winnebago. We start the reduction sequence. It's a five-stage sequence. We run the first four stages here in the mother machine, but we hold off on the fifth stage. You step out of this machine here—still at normal size. The fifth-stage sequence along with the specifications of your physiology and metabolic data will remain stored in the memory banks of the mother machine here.

"You, me, and two technicians get into the Winnebago mobile command post and drive Upstate. The drive will take a little over two hours. When we get there, we will secretly station ourselves within the target zone. That will be our jumping off point where we will launch the drone. The drone will be mounted on a launch pad on the roof.

"Remember at this point you're still at normal size. Now, you'll step into the remote unit. We will call the technicians back here at the warehouse and tell them to turn on the mother machine and ready it to transmit the final sequence. The mother machine will shoot the entire sequence by microwave transmission from an antenna on the roof of this place to an antenna on our Winnebago and that will activate the remote unit. Once it has all the transmitted data in its circuitry, the remote unit will complete the final, fifth sequence of the reduction process. In less than ten minutes you will be reduced to six inches."

Max continued, "At this point we will lift you to the roof launch pad where you'll position yourself on the drone. The drone will take to the air, and our technician will guide it to the target building. After the drone has landed on the roof, you get off the drone and go into the building."

Jake listened to this explanation without saying a word. He stood there silently absorbing, digesting, and evaluating all that Max was saying. To Jake it seemed like an outlandish plan. It all hinged on whether this behemoth machine and the remote unit really could deliver the goods and reduce a full-grown human being to miniature size. Jake was skeptical, but Max said that the technicians had tested the process on six volunteers and it worked, so maybe the plan was feasible.

"What about roof sensors? Will the drone trigger them?"

"We don't think there are sensors on the roof. Our ground observers watched whenever there was any roof activity. Security guards never appeared. We concluded that the roof is not wired, or if it is, it would take a larger object than this drone to set them off. As long as you're tiny you don't have to worry about sensors."

"How will I get inside?"

"Through an HVAC vent on the roof. You'll climb down in a vent air duct to the floor where the main computer and transmitter are located. We will provide you with special suction handles that will enable you to grip the walls of the duct so you can lower yourself down."

Jake nodded; it seemed that the strategic planners at BRIA had thought of everything—maybe.

"When you're on the designated floor, you'll make your way to the computer room, locate the transmitter and plant our bugs in the circuitry. We will be able to trace your movements and we will be in constant radio contact to guide you in case you get lost or deviate from the target. After you plant the bugs, you'll make your way out the way you came in. When you get back on the roof and climb onto the drone, it will fly you back to the Winnebago where we will be ready to assist your landing. We will wait for you to grow back to your normal size, then we'll drive back to Manhattan. Mission accomplished!

"And there it is Jake. As you can see, everything has been carefully thought out. The strategic planners have devised the perfect, master plan. They thought of everything. Nothing can go wrong. You'll be so small that you'll be able to get into the building and move about without anyone seeing you or without you setting off any alarms. You'll be in and out in less than thirty minutes, and we'll make a clean getaway. The geeks will never know that anyone came and went or tampered with their hardware. It will be a cinch, a piece of cake for you. It will be like a walk in the park. No sweat.

"Well, Jake you've heard the plan. You know what's involved. Are you in or out?

Max looked expectantly at Jake. Jake didn't answer at once. He stood thinking about all that Max had said. He considered the stages of the mission and how the plan would work to pull everything together to accomplish the objective.

He imagined himself as a miniature, doll-like man flying on the toy drone and landing on the roof of the building. He pictured himself entering the enemy fortress, lowering himself down the air ducts to the lower floor, then making his way through the corridors of the building looking for the computer room. Once he got into the computer, he would navigate through the circuitry and plant the bugs in the transmitter.

He mentally went through the escape scenario, visualizing his miniature self, retracing the path to get back to the roof, then mounting the drone and flying back to the Winnebago remote unit.

He asked himself what it would be like to be a mouse-man sneaking through enemy territory. He tried to anticipate potential dangers that might he encounter and how he would deal with them if he were only six-inches tall. *Would being small make him so innocuous that he could move about without being noticed? Or would his diminutive size make him more vulnerable should he encounter an adversary?*

"What about the personnel in the building?' he asked, "What if I run into someone?"

"You'll go in late Saturday night. Our agents report that there is only a skeleton crew at that time. It is unlikely that you will run into anyone. Maybe there might be a lone custodian doing some late-night cleaning, but otherwise the upstairs floor, the one with the computer and transmitter, will be deserted. And on the off chance that you do see anyone, you'll be so small that you can hide in a corner or under a desk. No one will see you."

Jake nodded. Max sounded so confident, so sure that the job would go off without a hitch. But, of course, it was easy for him to be confident because he wouldn't be the one reduced to doll size. He wouldn't have to enter the enemy's den and face the potential threats of exposure, capture or death. No, all that would be left to Jake.

Jake reviewed the details of the operation in his mind. On the surface it seemed that the strategic planners had thought of everything. *It would be a cinch, a piece of cake. Like a walk in the park.* Jake snorted; he had heard all that before. In the planning stage everything is perfect. On the drawing board everything has been carefully worked out to the last detail; but Jake had learned from experience that things were different in the field. He recalled his experience on a mission when he had to take a leak on the premises: no one in *Strategic Planning* has considered that contingency. And that was only a minor incident. This time Jake would be entering a virtual fortress where the geeks could possibly be inside. The stakes would be higher, the mission more complicated, and the chances of encountering the unexpected would be greater.

Jake was aware that the master minds in *Strategic Planning* are only human beings. They may act like they are omniscient but they have their limitations. They can't see into the future and they can't plan for unexpected contingencies. They have no way of knowing what the enemy is thinking, where he is lurking, how much he knows, nor can they anticipate how the enemy will respond when he discovers an intruder who sneaks into his lair.

Yes, in the beginning, the plan is always perfect, until it's not. Nothing can go wrong, until it does. There will be no snags, until there are. On paper the plan is perfect, but in the field, nothing is certain. That's what makes field operations so dangerous; there is always something that comes out of the dark to scuttle the perfect plan. There is always some unanticipated flaw that springs up from nowhere to upset the apple cart. There are always unseen enemies that lurk in the shadows. Even the best strategic minds cannot plan for the unexpected, the unknown, and the unseen.

At the beginning of every operation, the strategic planners always think that they have devised the foolproof plan, but perfection is an elusive quality and foolproof planning often evaporates when it confronts reality. In the final analysis it all comes down to the realization that planning can only do so much, after that, it's all up to the imagination and capabilities of the field agent. Each agent must peel his own banana, and with this mission the banana would be larger than any that he had encountered before.

Jake tossed all these thoughts around in his mind as he put all the pieces of the plan together. He considered the pros and cons of the entire operation. He thought over all the information that Max had put before him. He imagined the potential risks and tried to predict his chances of success. In the final analysis, after all his mental gymnastics and calculations, he was left with only his gut feeling and his instincts. He realized that nothing is certain and life is a gamble; all you can do is pay your money and take your chances. And Jake knew from experience that is what espionage is all about: playing the stakes and hoping for the jackpot. At that point, he turned to Max and said simply, "I'm in!"

Max beamed with spontaneous delight. "Wonderful Jake! I'm glad that you're on board and a member of our team. I was sure that once you saw how important this objective was, you would want to get in on the ground floor of this mission. I sensed that you were a man who relishes any and all challenges and takes pride in overcoming them. I felt sure that you would be charged with enthusiasm once you saw the exciting new technology that we had developed. Moreover, I just knew that your sense of duty and your patriotic pride would inspire and motivate you to tackle this most necessary objective. I must say that I'm pleased, even overjoyed, that you are part of the team. Now, I know that we will succeed and accomplish the objective with flying colors. Yes, with your extensive field experience, your resourcefulness in the face of adversity, and our technical expertise, success is all but guaranteed."

"Okay Max, enough!" said Jake. "Cool your jets, shift your enthusiasm into low gear and take your foot off your emotional accelerator. What's next?"

"Cool your jets, shift into lower gear, emotional accelerator! Jake you have such creative metaphors. It is so delightful listening to you and hearing your imaginative expressions. You have no idea how much I—"

"Enough Max, enough! Stop before you have an orgasm. Just tell me what's next."

"What's next, yes I was coming to that. I'll have you talk with Oliver Vinick. You know him?"

"Yes, vaguely. He's in *Ordnance and Equipment*, isn't he? Yeah, we worked together a while back."

"Well, he will be up here around two. He will show you the devices that you'll install and go over the equipment that you'll use on this assignment. I think you'll be impressed with the stuff that the guys in *O & E* have put together for this job.

"Until then, it's lunch time. Go out and have a long, leisurely lunch then come back before two, then Oliver will go over all the details."

Jake nodded. He went downstairs and exited the warehouse and walked out to the sidewalk. He looked at his watch. It was a little after noon. That gave him almost two hours to eat. He walked to Fourteenth Street, turned left then walked East. He was looking for a restaurant, not a fast-food joint, but nothing fancy. He wanted to find someplace that was quiet and not crowded so he could think and digest all the information that Max had just presented.

He got to Seventh Avenue and looked to his left and right. He didn't see any food places that captured his attention. He continued to walk. When he got to Sixth Avenue, he looked to his right and saw a small place just past Thirteenth Street and he walked over to it. The sign above the window read, *Bar Six*. Jake walked over to it to check it out. From the outside, it seemed appealing so he walked inside. He went to the back and was delighted to find that the dining room was small, quiet, and cozy. It had the atmosphere of a European bistro. It seemed an ideal place to have a sedate lunch.

Jake seated himself a small table by the wall. When the waitress came over, he ordered the French roast beef dip and a side of fries. While he was waiting for his food to arrive, Jake mulled over the strategy for *Operation Dense Fog*. On the surface it seemed like the entire operation had been well-thought out and carefully planned. Yet, Jake had the gnawing feeling that something had been overlooked, that somewhere there was a hidden fly in the ointment, a glitch. He couldn't identify the glitch, but maybe in time, with more thought, it would come to him.

After lunch Jake returned to the Warehouse and walked up the stairs to the fourth floor and then down the hall to Max's office. Max welcomed Jake with his usual high-octane greeting.

"Hi Jake! Good timing. I just spoke to Oliver. He's already up on the fifth floor in the room with the drone and the mother machine; the same room that we were in this morning. He said that he has the equipment already laid out and he's ready to go over it with you."

"Aren't you coming up?"

Max shook his head. "No, you don't need me for this. When you two are done talking, come back to my office and you and I will set up our schedule for the week."

Jake nodded, left Max's office and took the elevator to the fifth floor. He entered the drone room and saw a man arranging some things on a long table against the wall.

"Oliver?"

The man turned and faced Jake. "Yeah, that's right. You're Jake Barrada. We worked together before, didn't we? How long ago was it?"

"About a year, I think. Good to see you again."

"Likewise. If you step over here I'll show you the stuff that we've created for your assignment. Let's start with the drone. It's small and light weight. The body is of anodized aluminum with a dark-gray, matte finish so the craft will not reflect light. It will blend in with the night sky and make it almost invisible to the naked eye.

"Note that the body contours of the drone are all angular allowing radar waves pass over and around and not reflect back to any radar screens. In addition, the surface is coated with semi-conducting polymers that will absorb a portion of the radar beams making this craft undetectable to radar waves.

"The motors are all electric, so they are virtually silent. In addition, they are enclosed in an insulating material which blocks infrared radiation and makes them undetectable to heat sensors.

"All this means that you'll be flying to *Dense Fog* on a drone that is virtually invisible to the human eye and undetectable to radar, sound and heat sensors.

"Now if you'll follow me over to this table I'll show you what we created for you."

Jake followed Oliver Vinick to another table.

"Let's start with the body suit." Oliver held up a sleek, black, one-piece garment. "This is what you'll wear. It's elastic and has properties similar to bomb cloth. It's super tough and impervious to knife slashes."

"Is it bullet proof?"

"No, but even if it were, it wouldn't help you. If a bullet hit your six-inch frame, it wouldn't have to penetrate. The impact of the slug would be enough to pulverize your body and send you into orbit. Your best defense against a gunman will be to stay hidden. If you are discovered, keep moving. It would take an extraordinary marksman to hit a six-inch moving target."

"The suit looks kinda small," asked Jake. "Are you sure it will fit?"

"Positive. It will stretch to fit your torso and there will be no loose cloth to get caught as you squeeze through narrow spaces. In addition, it's made of totally organic fiber developed by R & D, so it will shrink and grow as you do. That may not seem like much, but it's an impressive achievement when you consider that not all cloth will reduce in the machine."

Oliver chuckled. "We had a woman who volunteered to go into the reduction machine. The process worked perfectly on her. She shrunk, but not her clothes. When we opened the door to the reduction chamber, there she was, a six-inch naked woman standing in the pile of her oversized clothes. We gave her a Kleenex to wrap around herself.

She had to wait an hour to grow back to her normal size before she could put on her clothes.

"But that won't happen with this bodysuit. We sent it through the machine. It reduces perfectly and it will expand with you as the reduction process wears off and you grow back to normal. By the way, you won't need underwear with this suit. The crotch is lined with soft, absorbent, cotton-like material that will pad and cuddle your family jewels."

"Seems like you guys have thought of everything."

"We like to think so. Next, we come to the boots. They're made of the same material as the body suit. The boots are three-quarter to wrap around your ankles and give you firm support when you're moving about and climbing. The soles are made of an organic material similar to rubber. They have treads and suction cups to grip even the smoothest surfaces and give you maximum traction in case you have to move fast.

"Over here are the gloves. Same material as the suit. The palms and fingers are padded to give you a good grip even on smooth, polished surfaces. The knuckles have these hard discs for protection and provide a good punch, like brass knuckles."

"I don't imagine that I'll have much of a punch when I'm not much bigger than a mouse."

Oliver shrugged. "Maybe not, but they are there if you should need them. Here is the hood. It will cover your neck, chin, ears and head. It's fitted with a communication device that will enable you to stay in touch with the remote command post. The unit is powered by a flexible lithium battery that is built into the fabric of the hood. The speakers are in the ear pads and a mike is in the cheek pad."

"Okay," said Jake, "but when I'm mouse size won't my voice be very small, and will the reduced mike be able to amplify it so it can be heard at the other end?"

"Good question. The answer is yes. We've designed the battery so it will maintain power even when it's reduced. It should be able to keep the communicator signal strong for at least an hour."

"Will this device always be activated?"

"Naturally it will be when you're speaking, but if you stop talking for fifteen seconds it will automatically shut off. That's to conserve the battery. When you want to turn it on again there's an on-off button on the right cheek pad. All you have to do is tap it. You can also use the button to turn the communicator off if you find it distracting."

Oliver picked up two other items.

"These are the suction handles. You'll use these to climb up and down flat walls. To use them, press the handles against the wall surface. There are suction cups on either end of the handle. You enable the suction by pulling the trigger on the inside of the handle with your index finger. When you want to break the suction and release the handle, press the red button on top of the handle with your thumb. Go ahead, give them a try against the wall."

Jake picked up the two handles and walked over to the wall. He pushed one handle against the wall and pulled the trigger. The handle gripped the wall surface as if it had been spot-welded in place. He placed the second handle higher up on the wall and pulled the trigger. The handle held fast to the wall. Jake pulled himself up to the second handle, pressed the button to release the first handle which he positioned higher up, above the second handle. He enabled the suction on this handle and pulled himself up to the next height. He repeated the suction-climbing technique and was able to raise himself about two feet off the floor. At that point he pressed the red buttons, released the suction on both handles and dropped back to his starting position.

"Whew! These handles really work, but it takes a lot of strength just to go up a couple of feet."

"Yeah! No one said it would be easy. Technology can only do so much; after that, it's up to whatever strength you can muster. I imagine that your best bet would be to find cracks or projections on the wall to dig your feet into so you give support to your arms."

Jake looked at the other items on the table. "What are these things?"

"Ah, yes, those things. They are the reason for this whole operation. Those are the electronic transmitter bugs that you will plant into the computer circuitry in *Dense Fog*. They have clips that will connect them to the circuitry."

"Are these also made of organic material?"

"No, they are mostly graphene, silicon and some special metallic elements. Organic material doesn't conduct electrical impulses, nor does it have the strength and durability of the metallic stuff."

"Then why use organic at all?"

"Because it reduces and grows at the same rate as the human body. Metallic-silicon is somewhat slower. Consequently, we used organic for all the wearables such as the suit, boots, gloves and hood. We made the other items out of the metallic material. These things will reduce and enlarge but slowly, not at the same rate as the human body or the organic stuff."

"Okay, I'll take your word for it. What else?"

"This is the backpack that you'll wear to carry the suction handles and the transmitter bugs. Here is a headlamp the you'll wear to light your way when you're crawling around in HVAC ducts, and when you're searching around in the computer circuitry."

At this point Oliver unrolled two large paper plans. "Finally, here are two layouts. This one is a floor plan of the inside of the building. It shows where you have to go to find the big computer and transmitter. The other is an internal circuit plan of the computer and transmitter unit. You can see here on the schematic where you will connect the transmitter bugs. You won't be able to take these with you so you'll have to memorize both plans."

"Why?" asked Jake. "Won't they reduce?"

"The paper will, but the graphics on the surface close up and get all jumbled and unintelligible when reduced. We tried everything but nothing works. There is no way around it; you'll have to memorize the plans."

Oliver looked back at Jake and said, "well, that's about it. Any questions?"

"One. *Surveillance* thinks that there are no sensors on the roof, but suppose they're wrong. Suppose there are motion sensors and heat sensors in the building and on the roof; will my activity and body heat set them off?"

Oliver shook his head. "No, not when you're miniature size, but if you get bigger then you will activate any sensors that might be there."

"How much bigger before I set off any sensor alarms?"

"That's hard to say. Depends upon how the sensors are calibrated. I would imagine that if you grew to be about the size of a child you would trip them. But you don't have to worry. *Strategic Planning* predicts that you'll be in and out of *Dense Fog* in about twenty minutes—half-hour tops. You won't start growing in that time. Anything else?"

Jake looked at all the stuff on the table before him. He shook his head, "No, I think you've covered everything. Maybe I'll have questions after I've practiced using this stuff. If so, I'll come down to your office. Thank you, Oliver!"

Oliver nodded. "We in *O & E* think that we put together a really good package of sophisticated equipment, but a lot will depend on how you use it when you get into *Dense Fog*. Good luck!"

With that, Oliver left. Jake was alone to examine each piece of the equipment. As he picked up the items and studied them, he reflected on Oliver's words: *a lot will depend on how you use it when you get into Dense Fog.* As Jake considered those words, they brought him back to his previous thought: *planning can only do so much, after that, it's all up to the imagination and capabilities of the field agent.*

Jake spent the next hour handling and getting the feel for various pieces of equipment. Later he would try on the suit, shoes, gloves and hood and he would have to practice with the suction handles. Using the handles would be difficult but he was sure that in time he would be able to master the climbing and lowering technique. The two items that concerned him the most were the floor plan of the building and the computer circuit layout. He felt that he could memorize the plans as diagrams, as lines on a paper surface. But he wondered how would his memorized images of abstract linear schematics hold up when he was faced with the genuine thing? *Would the plans really guide him when he was a little mouse-man running through the canyons of the building corridors or would everything appear strange and totally unrelated to the paper diagrams?* Unfortunately, he really would not know the answer to that question until he actually entered the building and tried to find his way around the interior halls.

CHAPTER 9

Jake went downstairs to Max's office. Max was working at his computer, but he stopped work and looked up when Jake appeared.

"You saw all the equipment and paraphernalia? Did Oliver explain everything? You satisfied? Well of course, you must be. How can you not be satisfied? You have to admit that *O & E* has put together a nifty little package. And I have to admit that they never cease to amaze me with the stuff they come up with."

Max paused and Jake spoke before Max could get his verbal motor running again. "Yeah, it's all good stuff, now where do we go from here? What's our time table? When do we go for the target?"

"Ah, once again Jake cuts to the quick and zeros in on the point at hand. Always a man of action, that's our Jake. As to our schedule; that's largely up to you, it depends on how much time you need to familiarize yourself with the equipment and declare yourself ready to tackle the objective. Today is Monday; ideally, we'd like to get into *Dense Fog* this coming Saturday. That is, if you think that you'll be ready in a week's time, but I don't want to rush you. You take as much time as you need to get ready for this mission. Bear in mind, however, that the longer we wait, the greater the risk that—"

"Right, Max, I'm aware of what's at stake. I think that I can get my act together in a week. Let's plan on launching our balloon this coming Saturday. If I encounter any problems then we might have to delay our timetable, if so, I'll let you know."

"That's good Jake. I like your attitude. It shows that you're a real team player; ready to adapt and do whatever it takes to get the show on the road. Ever ready and always eager to tackle the objective and get into the thick of things. Always keeping your eye on the goal, your shoulder to the wheel—"

"Whatever you say, Max. I've done all I can today, so I'm going, but I'll be here bright and early every day starting tomorrow. See you then."

With that, Jake turned and walked out of the office before Max had a chance to say anything more. He walked to the stairwell, went downstairs, left the building and headed for the subway. He took the train to his regular stop and walked back to his apartment, but he stopped along the way for a bite to eat.

When he was back in the solitude of his private domicile, away from the high-tech environment of the BRIA warehouse and insulated from the people in the streets and stores below, Jake had time to reflect about what lay before him in the coming week and what it would take to meet the challenges of this new objective. Jake had gone out on many assignments in the past, but he had always tackled them as himself, moving through the world around him as a full-sized human being.

This time it would be different. This time he would be reduced to the size of a rodent moving about in a world of giants. He wondered how that would feel and how he would maneuver and cope in the enemy's lair as a six-inch man. Small size might be an advantage; he could keep out of sight by hiding in nooks and crannies and under furniture. But it would also be a major disadvantage if he was caught out in the open. It would make him very vulnerable if he had to face off against an adversary who would come at him like the mythological Gorgon.

In addition, that gnawing feeling that something had been overlooked, the glitch that he couldn't put his finger on, popped up at odd moments and caused him to wonder if there really was something that the masterminds had overlooked or was he just being superstitious.

These thoughts bounced around in mind every night when he was alone in his   apartment. They would continue to reverberate in his conscience right up to the moment when he reached the objective.

During the week, Jake was in the BRIA Warehouse every day. He started by donning the body suit, boots, gloves, and hood. Then he did a variety of physical exercises and calisthenics to test the flexibility and strength of the garments and see if they would restrict his movements in any way. He didn't encounter any problems; everything seemed ideal.

He practiced climbing up and down walls with the suction handles. The suction devices were highly effective, but Jake was painfully aware that these maneuvers required a great deal of muscular strength—strength that he didn't have. If he was going to climb through the HVAC system he would have to find toe holds to help relieve the stress on his shoulders and arms as he moved up and down.

He turned his attention to the communicator in the hood and tested it by engaging in a radio dialogue with a technician in the Winnebago. Communication was loud and clear, but he was aware that now he was well within the range capability of the system and his voice was normal volume.

When he reached *Dense Fog*, he would be at least six miles away from the Winnebago and only six-inches tall. *Would the communication system still be effective at that distance transmitting his tiny mouse-voice? And when he actually got inside the building would he still be able to communicate with the outside world or would the thick walls of the structure stifle radio transmission? O & E* assured him that the communicator would function perfectly, but the real answer to those questions would only come when he was actually on site in the field. For now, all he could do is hope for the best.

Testing the equipment was relatively easy. Memorizing the floor plans of the building and electrical schematic of the target computer proved to be more of a challenge. After studying the plans for over an hour, Jake found that his mind was cluttered with a jumble of dense lines, angles, symbols and obscure technical nomenclature. He was unable to translate the flat plans and schematics into three-dimensional space because he could not visualize the interior maps and circuit diagrams as anything more than meaningless patterns on a flat piece of paper. To him they were more like Mondrian abstractions than actual corridors and rooms or electronic components. It seemed like he was facing an impossible challenge.

In desperation, he went downstairs to the computer department and asked one of the artist-technicians in the graphics unit if he could create a three-dimensional animation from the plans. The computer nerd assured Jake that he would be able to do that, and in almost no time, the artist-techie created an animation that allowed Jake to virtually navigate through the simulated interior of *Dense Fog* by manipulating the controls of the computer. It was as if the plans and diagrams had become a real three-dimensional environment, a place with a floor, walls and a ceiling, Jake now had a real feeling of what the interior of *Dense Fog* would be like when he got inside. Another animation of the electronic circuitry allowed him to virtually tour the inside of the computer, navigate through the components and locate the transmitter nodes where he would attach the spy-bugs.

Jake diligently practiced and studied for the next three days. On Thursday, Jake met with Max and announced that he would be ready to go on Saturday. Max smiled and nodded with obvious delight. They agreed that *Operation Dense Fog* would start at five on Saturday afternoon.

That Saturday, Jake arrived at the BRIA warehouse a little before five. He went directly up to Max's office. Max was busy working at his computer, but when Jake entered the office he looked up with a big smile and rose to greet Jake. He radiated the image of confidence and self-satisfaction; the project that he had worked on for the last six months was coming off the drawing board and was about to become a reality. Now he was obviously eager to get started.

"Are you ready Jake?"

"As ready as I'll ever be."

"Nervous?"

"No, I wouldn't say nervous. Anxious is more like it; and maybe a little apprehensive. I usually have feelings like this before any new assignment. Of course, this is a whole new ball game. I've never been shrunk to miniature size and I wonder what it's going to feel like. So maybe my anxious apprehension is mixed with a healthy dose of curiosity."

"Well," observed Max, "it's only natural to be curious and maybe a little apprehensive. Our volunteer test subjects all had similar feelings before then stepped into the machine. But, not to worry, your curiosity will soon be satisfied in due time. And I'm confident that once you have had time to adapt to your new size, your new being, you will marshall your inner resources to meet and overcome any problems that the situation might throw at you. Yes, whatever apprehensions that you may feel now will fade when you--"

"Whatever you say, Max. Let's go up to the fifth floor. I imagine that the technicians are waiting at the reducing machine."

Together Jake and Max took the elevator to the fifth floor and entered the room with the reducing machine. Two technicians were standing by. After the four men exchanged brief greetings, one of the technicians told Jake that he should change into the outfit that he was going to wear for the mission. Jake nodded and went out to put on the body suit, gloves, boots and hood. Thus, properly attired, he returned and announced that he was ready to proceed.

The technician nodded and opened the door to the machine. Jake stepped in and examined details of the interior. It was a small chamber, not much bigger than an old-fashioned telephone booth. The walls had a grid pattern of three-inch squares. There was a bench attached to the back wall.

Jake turned to the technician.

"Should I stand or sit down for this?" he asked.

"Doesn't make any difference. We're only running the first four stages of the sequence. You won't be reduced. That will come later, when you're in the remote unit in the Winnebago. At that point you may want to stand. If you sit on the bench you may feel like you're sitting on the edge of a cliff when you get reduced. That might feel a little unnerving and it could be awkward if you slipped off. You ready?"

Jake nodded. The technician shut the door and Jake was alone within the confines of the narrow chamber. He waited, wondering what would come next and what he would sensations he would feel. The ceiling, a panel of translucent, white plastic, lit up with a soft light. Then there was a steady hum with occasional beeps and clicks, but not much else. It sounded like he was listening to a vacuum cleaner running in another room. Jake waited; he looked at his hands and feet and felt his arms. As far as he could tell there was no difference. He couldn't see or feel any change. If the machine was running the reducing sequence, it didn't seem to be affecting him. Jake continued to stand there in the soft mellow light, waiting for something to happen--some change to occur--but there didn't seem to be any difference. Everything remained the same.

After a few minutes the humming noise stopped, the ceiling light went out and all was quiet. The door opened and Jake was greeted by the stoic technician.

"Okay, that's it! We're done here. You can join your team and be on your way."

"That's it? That's all? I didn't feel a thing. Are you sure it worked?"

The man nodded. "Pretty sure. You won't feel any different until you're in the remote unit and we run the final sequence. That's when the big change--or in this case, little change—will happen. That's when you'll feel yourself getting smaller and the world getting bigger."

Jake stepped out of the chamber and started toward Max, but he stopped and turned when a sudden thought occurred to him. He looked at both the technicians who were still standing in place by the controls of the reducing machine.

"Have you guys tried this remote sequencing before? I mean with somebody going through the first part of the sequence here, then sending the final stage to the remote unit miles away? Have you tried that and if so, did it work?"

"Sure," said one of the technicians. "We tried it a couple of times and there were no mishaps."

The other guy added, as a kind of footnote, "Although, we only experimented by sending the signal short distances, no more than fifty miles. You'll be going Upstate farther than that, but we're sure that we have enough power to transmit our signal that distance and beyond if need be. So, it should work out exactly as planned. But if it doesn't, call us and we'll try to figure out something."

Both men nodded and displayed a look of confidence and assurance, but Jake was a little skeptical at what seemed like cavalier indifference on their part. As he looked from one man to the other, he wondered if they were as certain of this procedure as they appeared to be, or if they were putting on an act for his benefit. He was about to probe deeper when Max put his arm around Jake's shoulder.

"Ahh! Come on Jake, there's nothing to worry about. These guys know what they're doing. R & D always comes through. Everything'll be fine and dandy. Now let's get a move on. Time's a-wastin and we got a long drive ahead of us."

Jake allowed himself to be led by Max from the room. As they were walking out, Jake thought about all he had just heard. The technicians and Max seemed so sure, so confident that this reducing procedure and the remote sending signal would work to perfection. Yeah, but they didn't have to go through the reducing procedure. They wouldn't be two hours Upstate away from the safety and security of the main *R & D* facility. At this point everyone was confident and sure that everything would work out according to plan—everyone except Jake, who still harbored nagging doubts. If there was a malfunction, it would be Jake who would face the consequences.

Jake and Max took the elevator down to the ground floor and went to the garage. There in the garage was the Winnebago with two men standing beside it. Max walked over to them.

"Jake, I want you to meet the other half of our team. This is Peter. He's our driver. He'll be driving our vehicle Upstate to the jumping-off point. This is Spike. He's gonna be inside our command center with me. He will operate the remote unit of the reducing machine for the fifth stage. Then when you're miniature size he'll carry you to the roof and help you mount the drone. He'll be at the controls to pilot the drone when you fly from the Winnebago to the roof of *Dense Fog*. Once you're inside, he'll follow your movements with the tracking system and guide you to your target. He will be in constant communication with you every step of the way and warn you if you're going astray."

Max stepped back and assumed a pontifical attitude.

"Okay men," he said, "we're ready to begin our grand adventure. I must say that I have good vibes about this. I feel that we are about to embark on a new and exciting adventure, one which goes beyond the current boundaries of science and technology and utilizes the genius of the best creative minds in BRIA. With this advanced technology at our disposal, and with us working together as an efficient and dedicated team, I am confident that we will soon be on the road to completion of a successful mission that is destined to soar to Promethium heights. We should all feel a large measure of pride that we were the ones chosen to execute this vital and important mission. A mission that is vital to the safety and security of the United States of America. We are about to strike a blow for freedom and justice in this great country of ours. So, let's get into our vehicle and be on our way. From now on, it's one for all and all for one. It's damn the torpedoes, full speed ahead!"

Max was full of energy and vigor, obviously excited about going out on this new adventure. He wanted to radiate that energy and electrify the three men standing before him and charge them with enthusiasm for the task that lay before them; but his motivational speech fell on deaf ears. Jake, Peter and Spike remained stoic, without any visible signs of emotion—almost to the point of being blasé about the entire enterprise that they were about to undertake. To them this was a job to be done, not a thrilling, patriotic adventure in fantasy land. Max's exuberant fanfare had no effect on either Peter or Spike.

But Max's over-the-top soliloquy struck a chord in Jake and all of a sudden Jake realized what the glitch was that was gnawing at his psyche. At that moment, Jake realized that the elusive fly-in-the-ointment was Max Beltrane. *Operation Dense Fog* was a serious and potentially dangerous mission, but Max treated it as if it was going to be a patriotic Boy Scout hike in the woods. Jake suspected that Max was not completely grounded in reality, but it was as if he was living in some graphic adventure novel, and Jake wondered if Max's romanticized attitude would have serious consequences later on. Unfortunately, they were too far into the mission for Jake to voice his doubts.

Max did not see the wary look in Jake's eyes because he was expecting a hearty response from the three men, but they remained stoic and unmoved by his high-minded rhetoric. In fact, they appeared to be completely indifferent to his ebullient words. He considered launching into another spirited oration but before he could say anything, Peter walked around to the driver's side of the Winnebago, opened the door and climbed into position behind the steering wheel. Spike opened the side door and entered the interior. Jake walked to the front of the vehicle and opened the door to the passenger side. He was about to step up into the seat when Max called out to him.

"Oh Jake," Max cried, "I thought that you would want to ride in the back here with me. That way, we could talk on the way to the launch point. I was looking forward to discussing the mission, reviewing our plans and having some really quality conversation."

Jake thought to himself that the very last thing that he wanted to do was sit across from Max and carry on a bloated conversation during the two-hour drive ahead of them. Most likely the conversation would be more like one of Max's tedious, long-winded, didactic monologues rather than a meaningful dialogue and Jake shuddered at the prospect.

"No Max, you talk to Spike," he replied. "If it's all the same to you, I'd rather sit in the front next to Peter and see where we're going. I also want to think about what I'm getting into. I need to condition my thoughts by focusing on my plan of action. I don't want any distractions to affect my concentration."

With that, Jake climbed into the cab on the passenger side and shut the door. Max was left standing alone without an audience and he was obviously disappointed, but Jake didn't care. The part he said about focusing and conditioning himself up was just an excuse, something off the top of his head said to distance himself from Max's endless chatter. What he really wanted to do was lean back during the drive and let his mind roam aimlessly in intellectual pastures. He didn't need Max to intrude on his mental sojourn. Max shrugged, entered the Winnebago and closed the door behind him.

Now that the team was enclosed within the vehicle, Peter activated his remote and the garage door rolled up. He started the motor and drove out of the garage then reactivated the remote to close the door behind them. He piloted the Winnebago to the West Side Highway and drove north to the George Washington Bridge and crossed over into New Jersey. They were on their way and *Operation Dense Fog* was about to begin.

CHAPTER 10

For the first twenty minutes, Jake watched the road and occasionally glanced over to see how Peter was doing. Peter effortlessly maneuvered the Winnebago along the highway through the evening traffic. Satisfied that Peter was a confident and skillful driver and that he knew the way to the jumping-off point, Jake settled back in the passenger seat. He was no longer interested in the route they were taking, the sights along the way or the myriad other distractions of the drive. Instead, he closed his eyes and allowed his thoughts to drift.

His first thoughts were about *Dense Fog*. He reviewed the plan and envisioned the tactics he would employ to accomplish the objective. He tried to anticipate the possible challenges that lay ahead and the potential risks that he might encounter. He knew this assignment would be different from his previous ones. Of course, every assignment is different in one way or another from the one that went before. The objectives, execution, and challenges are never exactly the same.

But this time the mission would be unlike any that he had encountered before. He would have to secretly enter the enemy stronghold—a virtual fortress—through a ventilation shaft make his way to the computer, navigate the circuitry and plant the bugs. He would have to accomplish this without setting off any alarms or rousing the enemy geeks. Moreover, this time he would be going into action as a miniature man, a vest pocket agent—more like a combination of man and rat. And he wondered if he would be able to function on a diminutive level.

Then he had another thought: in addition to getting into the stronghold he would also have to get out. Jake recalled the model and satellite images of *Dense Fog*. The place was constructed with fences, barriers, sensors, and vicious dogs—all designed to keep intruders out. But that cuts both ways; those obstacles could also make the place a prison and keep an intruder from escaping. As he mulled all of this over in his mind, he wondered if he would be able to get in, accomplish his mission then get out when the time came.

Then Jake remembered something that Phil Niekrom had told him; he said that *Operations* had lost two agents on the previous assignments. They disappeared and no one knew what had happened to them. Jake wondered if this might be his fate this time around.

This, however, was not a thought that Jake wanted to dwell on. He knew that if he attached too much importance to the prospect of failure then he might lose his nerve and botch the whole operation by being insecure and overcautious. Timing would be essential; he only had about an hour to complete the entire mission and he would have to move swiftly and surely if he wanted to do the job and survive. Better not to overthink the mission lest negative thoughts cloud his judgement.

So, he dismissed all thoughts of the upcoming mission and allowed his mind drift into other cerebral pastures; he began to muse on the past. He asked himself how he ever came to work for BRIA in the first place. *What was it that attracted him to this kind work? Was he looking for a career or did he believe all that flag-waving patriotic rhetoric about keeping America safe from nefarious* enemies? No, these were never serious considerations because Jake came to realize that there was never a defining moment when he made the decision to get into clandestine espionage. It was as if he just got swept up in the currents of time and circumstance.

As the past unfolded in his mind, it occurred to Jake that his entire life seemed to an amalgam of unrelated, meaningless events that shaped his destiny without him being aware, at any one time, of what was happening or what was coming. So, without ever realizing it, he drifted aimlessly in life, moving closer and closer to BRIA until, at one point he was in, a full player on the team. It was almost as if he had been sucked into the organization by the invisible currents generated by the whirlpool of fate.

Now, sitting in the front seat of the Winnebago riding along the Upstate highway on the way to *Operation Dense Fog*, he felt that even now the mysterious forces of fate and circumstance were pulling him toward a strange and possibly dangerous assignment that would be unlike anything that he had ever experienced in his entire life and he wondered if he was up to the challenge. He wondered what fate had in store for him.

As the Winnebago proceeded north toward the objective, Jake interrupted his mental meanderings to look up at the road ahead and take in the surroundings. He judged that they had been traveling for about an hour and now they were well out of the city limits. The scenery had changed from urban cityscape to rural country side then to dense backwoods wilderness. It was still light out, but the sun was low on the horizon and it would soon be dusk. Most likely it would be dark before they arrived at the jumping off point. They continued their journey with Peter totally focused on driving and Jake allowing his mind to wander until at one point, Peter announced, "We're almost there".

Jake looked up at the road ahead. By now they were enclosed in total darkness; the only light came from the Winnebago headlights on the desolate road ahead. It was as if the very forces of nature had closed in on them. They drove for about ten more minutes then Peter pulled over to the side of the road, cut the engine and turned off the headlights.

"This is it. We're here," he said.

Jake looked through the windows. "Are you sure? It's black as pitch out there. I can't see anything. How can you be certain that we're in the right place?"

"I was with a scouting party that came up here a couple weeks ago. When we selected this site, we put markings on the trees. You can't see them now because it's too dark, but I saw them in the headlights as we drove up. We're in the right place all right. Let's go back and join the others."

Jake got out and walked to the side door. He waited for Peter to come around, then he opened the door and the two of them stepped inside. Max and Spike were seated inside quietly murmuring about something. Actually, it looked like Max was doing all the talking with Spike feigning interest. Peter and Jake sat down and the four men lapsed into silence just looking at each other with nobody saying anything. There seemed to be a quiet tension in the atmosphere. Jake noticed that even Max seemed uncharacteristically subdued.

Jake broke the silence. "Shouldn't we get started?"

"We're waiting," said Spike.

"Waiting for what?"

"Waiting for the moon to rise above the mountains. There'll be a full moon tonight, and when it's high in the sky it will give you plenty of light to see where you're going."

"I thought that you were going to pilot the drone. Do you need moonlight to reach the target?"

Spike shook his head. "No, I'll be guiding the drone with satellite communications and watching your progress on a monitor down here, but you might want to see how you're getting to the target. The moonlight will give you a sense of direction and help you to keep your bearings. You'll see what's around you and you can pick out landmarks so you won't feel that you're flying blind. It will also illuminate the rooftop so when you get off the drone you can find your way around and locate the HVAC port."

Jake nodded. That seemed logical. The four men continued to sit in silence until, at last, Spike looked out the window up at the sky. "The moon is up, it's time to get started."

Jake stood up and looked around. "Where's my backpack?"

"It's in the reducing machine. It went through the first four stages back at BRIA. When you step into the chamber, put it on, then we'll run the final stage."

Jake nodded, walked over to the reducing unit and opened the door. He saw his backpack on the bench. He entered the chamber, picked up the backpack and put it on, then he turned back to Spike and nodded that he was ready. Spike shut the door and for a brief moment Jake was in silent darkness, but then the overhead ceiling panel lit up with a soft, diffuse light. An audible hum sounded with clicks and beeps, signaling that the machine was activated and the fifth and final stage of the reduction process was starting. Very soon Jake would condense and shrink to become a miniature human being. He waited, wondering how it would feel to have all your atoms squeezed to a fraction of their normal size.

The machine was humming, clicking, beeping and Jake felt a slight tingling sensation, a subtle stimulation as if someone was running a vibrator over his body. Other than that, he didn't feel any different, but when he looked at his left hand resting against the grid pattern on the wall, he could see the metamorphosis happening. His fingers and palm were getting smaller and sliding down along the wall; at the same time the grid pattern appeared to be growing larger and rising higher. Jake glanced around at the interior of the cubicle. Everything was growing. Space was expanding. The ceiling was moving higher up away from him. The floor seemed to be rising and the walls were pushing away. He was getting smaller and the world was growing larger. He estimated that he was about half his normal size, then a quarter size, then smaller and still smaller.

A few more minutes passed. The humming ceased and the chamber was quiet. The final stage of the reduction process had ended. Jake was now a diminutive creature, a small being, a miniature rodent-sized human standing close to the floor looking up at everything around him. It was a strange feeling to be so low to the floor and see everything so far away. Before the reducing process revved up, the chamber was tight and narrow with little room to maneuver. Now it was more like the Grand Canyon, a vast space with the walls far away and a high, distant ceiling. He had entered the Lilliputian world of Gulliver!

The chamber door suddenly opened and Max appeared like a giant in the door frame. He looked down at Jake.

"Oh, Jake," he exclaimed, "how cute you look. How adorable! Just like a little mouse. If only you could see yourself!"

Jake felt self-conscious and vulnerable and he sensed an undertone of playful mockery in Max's exuberant exclamations. He let out a caustic barrage of profanities. Unfortunately, Jake's voice was tiny and the force of his invective was lost on Max.

Max was thoroughly enjoying Jake's doll-like stature and would have launched into more cutesy, saccharin commentary but Spike appeared and nudged him out of the way. Spike carried a small wire basket which he placed on the floor next to Jake.

"Here," he said, "climb into this and I'll carry you up to the roof."

Jake dutifully climbed over the rim and settled in the center of the basket. Spike picked it up by the handle and carried it from the chamber to an interior ladder. He climbed the ladder and emerged through a hatch to the roof of the Winnebago. On the roof was the drone, its wings and fuselage of black anodized aluminum barely visible even in the light of the full moon.

"Okay Jake, climb out and settle into the cockpit," said Spike as he held the basket against the fuselage of the drone. Jake maneuvered himself from the basket into the cockpit seat and fastened the seatbelt. While he was getting into position, Spike released the hold-down clips attached to the drone wheels.

"You ready Jake?" he asked.

Jake gave the double thumbs-up sign. He wasn't sure that Spike could see his miniature hands with only the moonlight for illumination, but Spike apparently saw and understood the gesture.

"Okay, turn on your communicator and I'll go down to the control panel and activate this thing. Soon you'll be up and on your way."

Spike descended through the hatch leaving Jake alone on the roof sitting in the cockpit of the drone. The full moon was high in the sky, its reflected light giving a ghostly aura to the atmosphere. The only sound in the stillness of the night was the medley of crickets chirping in the bush. He waited for something to happen and soon the propellers started to turn with a soft, steady whir. Then the drone lifted gently off roof and hovered above the Winnebago as if in a state of suspended animation. Jake was airborne.

Spike's voice came over the communicator. "Okay Jake, you should be about ten feet above the roof. You okay?"

Jake's voice came over the speaker in the Winnebago, "yeah, I'm fine."

"All right, hold onto the handles and I'll start you on your way. Next stop, the roof of *Dense Fog*."

The wing motors rotated from vertical to a horizontal position. The drone stopped rising and it quietly and effortlessly moved forward. The acceleration was so smooth and gentle that there was no sense of moving, no feeling of flight. Jake looked back and saw that the Winnebago was receding into the distance.

It was a calm night and the sky was clear. Jake looked up at the vast celestial canopy overhead, a tapestry of billions of bright stars sparkling against an endless black background, and he was transfixed by the grandeur of nature's cosmic masterpiece. As he gazed at the inverted bowl of black sky and twinkling stars above, he was suddenly overcome with the feeling that he had somehow merged with nature to become an integral part of the endless pattern of heavenly forces that are nature's boundless cosmos. He didn't know whether his miniature size—the smallest that he had ever been in his entire life—or whether being suspended in space away from any tangible reference points, produced this sudden, almost mystical feeling.

He only knew that in that moment he had transcended the physical bounds that had constrained him and he had the impression that he was being drawn from the bondage of life into the liberation that comes from a higher state of consciousness. He looked overhead and was captivated by wonderous sky above. He felt as if he had somehow been absorbed by the ethereal, spiritual presence of the limitless majestic universe.

The drone continued to glide forward but the flight was so smooth that Jake barely noticed that he was moving. He was lost in the moment and enveloped in a sublime feeling of tranquility. Time and circumstance had lost their relevance. That sublime feeling that comes with being lost in a vast realm without boundaries and without dimension, was abruptly interrupted by stark reality of Spike's voice.

"Okay Jake! You should be able to see the objective ahead and slightly to your left."

Jake awakened from his mystical cloud and was pulled back to the reality and purpose of his mission. He peered into the darkness ahead and saw a ring of spotlights in the distance.

"I see lights far away, but I can't make out anything else."

"You're still a couple of miles away so you can't see much, but keep your eyes peeled and soon you'll be able to make out the building and the fence."

The drone continued to fly silently toward the objective. Jake sat still in the cockpit with his eyes focused on the ring of lights in the distance. Slowly and silently, the drone moved closer to the target. Presently, Jake could make out the dark shape of the building and as he moved closer, he could see the surrounding fence and other features of the facility. The drone approached the high fence with its formidable coils of razor ribbon and flew over it. Jake looked down as the drone passed over the fence and crossed above the grounds around the building, and he saw the dogs below. They had grouped together as a pack and were looking up, watching the strange flying craft overhead and following its progress with their eyes.

"I'm just about over the roof," said Jake.

"I can see that on my monitor," replied Spike. "Get ready to come in for a landing."

The drone hovered over the roof and gently set down.

"Okay, Jake you should be on the roof. You can dismount the drone and make your way to the HVAC duct."

"I don't see it," said Jake. "I'm not sure where it is."

"Look around. You'll see a small structure with a door. I guess it looks kinda like a rooftop outhouse. That's the entrance port to the roof from below. You see it?"

"Yeah, I think so."

"Okay, then as you're facing the entry structure the HVAC duct will be to the left. You might not be able to see it from where you. Maybe it's in the shadows, but if you walk toward the entrance door you it should come into view."

Jake grabbed his backpack and climbed down from the drone and walked toward the dark shape that he assumed was the entrance structure. As he got closer to it, he could make out the details and see the door. Then he looked to the left and saw the HVAC vent.

"Okay, I see the vent."

"Fine," said Spike. "Now all you gotta do is climb into the opening then work your way down the vertical shaft to the first horizontal level. When you get there hang a left and walk to the first vent. That is where you climb out and you'll be in a supply room. Most likely it will be vacant at this time of night."

"Wouldn't it have been easier for me to stay my normal size then just go through the entrance door without having to crawl around in heating ducts?"

"No, Jake," cried Max who had been listening to the dialogue between Spike and Jake, "*Strategic Planning* worked out this method because they were certain that there would be heat sensors, motion detectors, surveillance cameras, and alarms monitoring the entrance way. Besides that, if you were big, then how would you get into the computer?

"No Jake, you must remember that when *Strategic Planning* devises a strategy, they consider the objective, evaluate all the factors involved, work out all the details and ultimately come up with the perfect foolproof plan. That is why we must follow their instructions to the letter and that is why—"

"Okay Max!" said Jake, "I don't need a lecture on the infallibility of *Strategic Planning*. Shut up and let me get on with the job."

Jake walked over to the HVAC vent, grabbed the top rim of the opening, pulled himself up and swung his feet into the wide aperture of the vent. He landed on a flat horizontal metal surface. This would be his jumping off point. He sat there while he pulled out the headlamp, gloves, and suction handles from his backpack. He turned on the headlamp and pulled the band around his head. He put on his gloves, then he attached the suction handles to the metal wall of the vent shaft. At that point he was ready to begin his descent. He took a couple of deep breaths, gripped the suction handles, kicked off his perch and began to work his way down into the secret interior of *Dense Fog*.

CHAPTER 11

Back in the Winnebago, Spike and Max watched the monitor to follow Jake's progress. The image on the screen showed a schematic of the building and a tiny white tracker blip. The tracker blip indicated Jake's location as he moved about. Suddenly the white blip went out.

"What happened?" asked Max with some anxiety. "The light went out. Where is he?"

Spike remained calm and unperturbed. "Most likely he's entered the air shaft and is completely surrounded by metal. The metal walls will block any signal. We won't know where he is until he comes out of the shaft. Then the signal will resume. In the meantime, all we can do is sit and wait for the signal to show up on the screen."

So, they sat there, eyes glued to the monitor. Spike was calm and stoic, looking at the screen as if he was watching tropical fish swim around in an aquarium. Max, however, was getting nervous—although he tried not to show it. He kept telling himself that there was nothing to worry about because all of this was part of *Strategic Planning's* perfect plan and nothing could go wrong. *Nothing could go wrong.*

Meanwhile Jake was slowly inching his way down the air shaft using the suction handles to lower himself inch by inch. It was tedious going and his arms were tiring. He tried to rest his arms by using his feet to push his against a wall and wedge himself in the shaft. With his back against one wall and his feet pushing against the opposite wall he was able to let go of the handles, drop his arms and shake off some of the fatigue that was setting in. Unfortunately, he was not able to maintain that position for long and he had to grab onto the handles and resume his downward descent.

Just when he was making steady progress and all seemed to be going well, he hit an unexpected pickle; he came to a certain section of the vent wall that was either coated with a film of oil or else was super slick. Whatever the reason, the suction handles suddenly lost their grip; Jake fell away from the wall and dropped into free fall down the shaft. He plunged straight down until the vertical shaft angled off. Jake hit that angle and his fall changed to a roll. He rolled down the angled shaft and eventually he popped out at a junction where he rolled onto a horizontal duct.

He lay on the flat metal surface for a few minutes while he tried to shake off the dizzying effects of his sudden downward roll. He had dropped the suction handles in his fall but they fell with him and slid down the angled shaft to land by his side. When he felt that he had recovered his senses, he sat up, put the handles in his backpack, adjusted his headlamp, and looked about to find a way out of the vent complex.

The horizontal duct was wide but not very high—not high enough for him to stand up—he would have to crawl on his hands and knees the rest of the way, but *which way? In what direction should he crawl to make his way out of the duct?* His original instructions were to go left when he emerged onto the horizontal level, but his rolling tumble completely disorientated him and now he wasn't sure of his directions. *Where was left and where was right?* Jake looked about. He was enclosed in a dark, tight, rectangular metal tunnel and he couldn't see beyond the beam of his head lamp. The four surfaces around him were of smooth, polished steel without any markings or clues to guide him.

Jake tried to mentally reconstruct the dizzy tumble that brought him to his present location but he couldn't be sure how many times he rolled over or when got turned around. The best he was able to do was make an educated guess as to his bearings and start crawling in the direction that seemed to be the left. He started to crawl through the darkness of the tight passage with only the narrow beam of his headlamp to light the way.

Soon he saw a dim light up ahead and he crawled to it. It was a vent port and it might offer a way out of the HVAC duct. When he reached the port, he found that it was closed by a metal grill. Jake positioned himself in front of the vent port, swung his legs around, put his feet against the grill and pushed. The grill was held in place with spring clips which yielded to the pressure that Jake brought to bear against it. He was able push it far enough from the vent to create a slim opening allowing him to squeeze through and drop down to the floor below.

The minute Jake dropped from the vent opening to the floor, the tracker blip lit upon the monitor screen that Spike was watching in the Winnebago.

"He's out," said Spike. "Jake is no longer in the air duct."

"Oh good!" said a relieved and buoyant Max, "now he can get on with the mission. It looks like the plan is coming together."

"Maybe not. Not yet," said Spike cautiously, "there might be a problem."

Max picked up on the tone of doubt in Spike's voice and his anxiety returned.

"What? What kind of a problem?" he asked.

"I'm not sure, but it looks like Jake came out of the air duct in the wrong place. I don't think he's where he should be," said Spike warily as he studied the screen.

"That's not possible! Jake was following the plan and the plan is supposed to be foolproof." Max was becoming increasingly agitated with this new development. "Well, if he's not where he's supposed to be, then where is he?"

"I can't tell. The floor plan on this screen is just an outline without enough detail. Hand me that paper on the desk." Spike turned around and pointed to a large schematic on the desk behind them. Max turned and quickly snatched up the paper and shoved it into Spike's hands. Spike held it up before the monitor screen and looked from one to the other trying to pick out the details on the paper schematic and match them to the outline on the screen.

"Well?" asked Max impatiently.

"As near as I can tell, Jake just entered the women's restroom."

"What?! What is he doing in there?"

"I don't know," replied Spike dryly, "Maybe he just dropped in to watch some broad come in and pull down her pants to take a dump."

Max was not amused. "This is no time to be funny, Spike. We are in the middle of an important mission and we may have hit a snag. This is serious. We have to remain focused on our goal and maintain constant, serious vigil, giving close, serious attention to Jake's progress if we are to see this to a successful conclusion. Let's have no more misguided attempts at sophomoric levity."

Spike shrugged his shoulders but said nothing.

Jake was standing on a tile floor and he saw immediately that there were metal stalls and toilet bowls. He looked at the walls and saw that there were no urinals. It was painfully obvious that he had taken a wrong turn, missed the supply room and landed in the women's toilet facility.

He tapped the contact in his right cheek pad to activate his communicator.

"Spike, this is me, Jake. Can you hear me?"

"Yeah Jake, I can hear you and I'm tracking you. It looks like you're in the women's restroom."

"Right! I figured that out by myself. How far am I from the computer room and how do I get there?"

"Okay, you're not too far from the computer room. To get there, first you gotta move out of the toilet into the hall."

As Jake was talking to Spike an unseen menace was creeping down the wall moving toward him. Jake was concentrating on his dialogue with Spike and was unaware of the creature that was silently closing in on him; then without warning it sprung from the wall and landed on Jake's back.

Jake was taken completely by surprise. He wondered what it was that had suddenly come from nowhere to attack him. He tried to reach over his shoulder and grab this unexpected phantom adversary, but the creature—whatever it was—managed to avoid Jake's grasp as it clung tenaciously to his back.

Jake had no idea what menace he was fighting with. In a desperate attempt to dislodge the mysterious attacker he spun around and pushed his back against the wall. That maneuver did the trick. The creature jumped off Jake's back and landed on the floor before him. Now Jake could see what had come out of the shadows to attack him. It was a large brown cockroach. It was the largest cockroach that Jake had ever seen; but then again, it may have only appeared especially large because Jake was relatively small.

To Jake it seemed like the vermin of the toilet had come out to attack him.

"Listen bug," he said in an attempt to reason with the roach, "I've got no beef with you, so back off and let me get the hell out of here."

Jake's tough words apparently fell on deaf ears—that is, if a cockroach even has ears—because the large insect came back at him. When the creature came within range, Jake shot a left jab, followed by a straight right to the part that he assumed was the roach's face. The insect backed off but was unfazed by Jake's blows. It seemed to be impervious to forceful punches. Jake wanted to kick the roach in the balls, but he wasn't sure if roaches have balls. *If so, where are they?*

The cockroach came at him again and Jake pushed it away. This was a frustrating struggle because the large insect was persistent in its attacks and nothing Jake could do seemed to deter the creature. He looked around for something that he might use as a weapon or some means of escape from this six-limbed beast. He spied a length of toilet paper hanging from a roll in the wall holder. Jake grasped the hanging paper and started to climb up. His weight caused the roll to unwind. Jake climbed faster and still faster with the result that he was able to reach the roll of toilet paper before it could completely unwind.

Back in the Winnebago Spike was intently watching the screen. He saw the locator blip bouncing up and down but it wasn't going anywhere. Something was happening. Spike didn't have a clue as to what Jake was doing but it appeared that he was stuck in the women's toilet. He tried to call Jake on the communicator but there was no response.

Max was looking over Spike's shoulder at the screen with impatient concern.

"Spike, what's going on? What is Jake doing? Where is he?"

"I donno. He seems to be stuck in the women's toilet. Something's going on, but I donno what."

"Can't you call him on the radio? Try doing that."

Spike shook his head. "I already tried to call him. He doesn't answer. We'll just have to wait to find out what's going on."

"Oh! This is terrible," cried Max with increasing impatience, "This isn't part of the plan. He was supposed to get into the building and go straight to the computer room, but now he's fooling around in the women's toilet. This isn't right. He has got to get out of there."

"Relax Max," said Spike, "Jake probably ran into some minor snag. We still got time yet. Let's just wait and see how he handles it."

That comment shut Max up but it didn't ease his anxiety.

Back in the women's toilet Jake was standing on the roll of toilet paper in the wall mount. The giant cockroach was down below, immobile, waving its antennae; it appeared that the roach was looking up, eyeing him from the floor. Jake looked down at the creature and wondered: *why was this giant bug attacking him? What did it want? Surely it wasn't going to eat him?* All Jake knew was that the cockroach was in his way and preventing him from his mission and he had to escape from it. *But what could he do? What action could he take?*

Well, he could wait until he grew back to normal size then he could simple step on the crusty insect and squash it into oblivion; but then he would be too big to get out and he would be trapped in the women's restroom, just waiting to be discovered by the enemy geeks and then he would be squashed into oblivion. In this game size was everything.

Jake looked over at the toilet bowl and he hatched a desperate, impromptu plan. If he could leap over to the bowl and walk around the rim, then he might be able to come down the opposite side and escape through one of the other stalls. He would have to leap from his perch on the toilet roll to the rim. If he slipped and missed, then he would fall to the floor and into the clutches of the cockroach or, on the other side, he might slide into the toilet bowl and drown in the water or get flushed away by the first broad that came in to take a whiz.

It was a daring plan but he decided to go for it. He took a deep breath and pushed himself away from the soft surface of the paper roll. He flew through space and landed, belly down, on the rim of the toilet bowl. The velocity of his leap caused Jake to slide across the slick porcelain of the rim toward the deep bowl and the water below. Fortunately, he was wearing gloves with super-grip palm pads and he was able to arrest his slip by pressing his hands down on the glassy ceramic surface of the rim.

Jake breathed a little easier because he thought that he had escaped the clutches of the cockroach but he hadn't reckoned on the relentless drive of the oppressive insect. He didn't know that cockroaches could fly, but this one could because it flew up to the toilet rim and landed on the prostrate Jake. Jake turned over and flung his arm around. He smacked the insect. The blow caught the creature off balance and it fell from Jake down into the toilet water. Jake looked down and saw the creature waving its six legs trying to tread water and stay afloat.

Jake realized that this was his chance. He ran along the rim and jumped up to grab the handle of the flush valve. His weight was enough to pull the handle down and activate the flush mechanism. There was a loud *swoosh* and Jake looked down to see the incoming water cascade down the sides of the bowl forming a whirlpool that captured and flushed the giant cockroach into the dungeons of the sewerage system never to return.

With the insect menace eradicated it was time to get out of the women's toilet. Jake used his suction handles to climb down the side of the toilet bowl. Then he made his way to the door of the restroom. The door was closed but there was a louvered vent at the base of the door. Jake pulled himself up to the vent and slid through the blades of the louver and he dropped down on the other side of the door.

He was now out of the restroom and in a hallway where he paused to collect his thoughts and consider his situation. He had done it; he had successfully navigated through the HVAC ducts, battled with a giant cockroach and emerged relatively unscathed into the hallway. Now he hoped that the most arduous tasks were behind him and that he could get on with the completion of his mission without further incident.

CHAPTER 12

Jake touched his cheek pad to activate the communicator.

"Spike, it's me. I'm out of the restroom and in the hall."

"I can see that," replied Spike. "What happened, why did it take you so long to get into the hall?"

"Never mind that now. It would take too long to explain and you wouldn't believe me anyway. Just tell me where I go from here and how I get to the computer."

"Okay, with your back to the restroom door, turn to your left and walk to the end of the hall. When you get there, turn to your right and go down that hall. You'll find the computer room at the far end. You got that?"

"Yeah! It seems simple enough. Left to the end of the hall then right and follow the hall to the computer room. I'm on my way."

Jake started walking, staying close to the wall and watching carefully for any surveillance cameras as he advanced. The hall was empty and quiet. He didn't see any cameras nor signs of life or activity anywhere.

Back in the Winnebago Spike was gazing intently at the screen, watching the blip showing Jake's progress; so far, he was moving in the right direction. Satisfied that Jake was on course, Spike turned back to Max.

"Okay, he's in the hallway making his way to the computer room. It should be easy from now on."

Max breathed a sigh of relief. Now he was confident that all the unexpected snags and uncertainties were past and that *Strategic*

Planning's perfect plan was coming together and nothing could go wrong. *Nothing could go wrong!*

Indeed, as Jake crept down to the end of the hall it seemed that everything was going according to plan, but when he turned right and looked ahead, he saw something that unnerved him. There, halfway down the hall, was a large orange cat. The beast was lying motionless on the floor with its head resting on one paw. Jake froze in place and studied the animal. It appeared that the cat was asleep, but Jake couldn't be sure from where he was standing because he was too far away to see if the cat's eyes were closed or not.

He stood still for a few moments and looked intently at the dormant animal watching for any telltale signs of movement, but the beast remained inert and motionless. The computer room was at the end of the hall and Jake wondered if he should risk sneaking past the sleeping cat to get to that room. *Suppose the beast should wake up when he tried to pass by it? How would it react to a miniature man passing by in front of him?*

He whispered into his communicator, "Spike, I'm at the end of the first hall. I've turned right and I'm looking at the computer room at the far end of this hall."

"I can see that," said Spike. "What's holding you up?"

"I may have run into an obstacle. Is this the only way into the computer room?"

When Max heard Jake say that he had run into an obstacle, he started to unravel.

"What?! He said that he ran into an obstacle. What sort of obstacle? There aren't supposed to be any obstacles. This wasn't in the plan. Ask him what—"

"Max! Will you be quiet. I'm trying to talk to Jake," said Spike glaring back at Max.

"Now, Spike," said Max with a hurt expression, "that's no way to talk to me. Show a little respect, after all I am in charge of this mission."

"All right Max," said Spike, "take charge of your mouth and keep it shut." Then Spike turned back to the monitor and said, "No Jake, that hall you're in is the only way to get to the computer room. You'll just have to try and get past whatever obstacle you're facing if you want to enter the computer room. I'll be watching your progress on the monitor."

Jake murmured a quiet "okay" then started to sneak down the hall. The cat was sleeping against one wall. Jake hugged the opposite wall, silently sneaking down the corridor on tiptoes—alert and on guard—intently watching the cat for any signs of movement. Closer and closer he advanced, being ever vigilant and ready to run should the orange tabby suddenly wake up. Soon he was almost directly in front of the feline figure which remained ostensibly dead to the world. As he advanced in front of the sleeping form, he was overwhelmed with how huge the beast was. The creature appeared to be an enormous tiger the size of a wooly mammoth.

Now he was directly across from the monster cat. He held his breath and made every effort to move as silently as possible. As he passed by the sleeping cat, Jake wondered what would happen if the animal suddenly woke up and saw him. *Would it remain passive and unconcerned with the tiny man that was creeping by or would it come alive and pounce on him? Would the cat recognize him as a small human being or would it see him as some sort of varmint to be captured and devoured?* Whatever, Jake did not want to find out the answer to those questions.

In two minutes—two minutes that seemed like an eternity—Jake moved past the sleeping cat and stood before the entrance to the computer room. He stepped inside. The room was dark. Jake switched on his headlamp. Then he called through to Spike.

"Okay Spike, I'm in the computer room facing the computer."

"Right! You know how to get inside the computer?"

"I think so; If I remember correctly, there are some ventilator ports on the side of this gigantic machine."

"Yeah, that's right. I've got a schematic on paper here before me. I'll try to guide you to the transmitter circuitry. According to this plan there is a service panel on either side of the computer. Go to the right side and find that panel. When you get there, you'll see the ventilator ports next to the panel. You want to through one of them. When you get inside call me to test our communication. It's possible that when you're inside the computer our signals will be cut off."

Jake went to the side of the big mainframe computer. He found the vent ports and climbed through one of them. When he was inside, he called to Spike,

"Okay Spike, I'm inside. Can you hear me?"

"Yeah!" replied Spike. "Your voice is a little weak but I can hear you."

"Good, now if I remember the circuit plan correctly, I'm supposed to climb up to the fourth level. That's where the transmitter modules are."

"That checks with my schematic. Is there anything you can climb up on?"

"The back panel is a perforated grid. I can climb up using the openings as a ladder."

"Well," said Spike, "go to it. According to this schematic there's a cooling fan on the fourth level. That should tell you that you're on the right level. Check back when you're there."

Jake approached he panel. He put one foot in a low opening and his hands in other openings above his head. He pulled himself up and started climbing. The openings were spaced at convenient intervals making it relatively easy to climb up the panel. In less than two minutes Jake was on the fourth level.

"Okay," he said, "I'm on the level. Now I think that all I have to do is walk across the horizonal circuit panels to find the transmitter modules."

"Yeah, that jives with the paper I have in front of me," said Spike. "You're almost there. The rest should be a cinch."

Jake walked carefully across the panels stepping gingerly across the integrated circuits and the components between them. He knew that he was getting close to the transmitter modules and he was confident that success was in his grasp, but when he looked at was before him he stopped because he saw another unanticipated stumbling block that he would have to deal with. It was a living, breathing obstacle that was not in *Strategic Planning's* perfect plan.

"Oh hell!" exclaimed Jake.

"What's the matter?" asked Spike.

"Jake," cried a worried Max, "what now? What's wrong?"

"There's a big gray mouse sitting right in front of the transmitter circuit. He's blocking the way. I can't get to the module nodes."

"Ah, come on Jake," said Max impatiently, "chase it away. After all, it's just a mouse."

"All right, I'll try."

Jake tried running at the creature, waving his arms about trying to make threatening gestures, but this had no visible effect on the rodent. The mouse raised up on its hind legs, bared its front teeth and extended its front paws, but it didn't budge. It remained steadfast in its place. Jake retreated.

"It's no use," he said with a sigh of frustration, "I can't chase it. I don't know whether he thinks that I want to fight or play with him."

"You gotta do something Jake!" barked Max, "that little rodent is holding up the works. It's preventing you from doing your job. Think of the mission. We've come too far to be stopped by a miserable little runt of a mouse. Show it who's boss. After all, what are you a man or a mouse?"

"Damn it, Max! Right now, I'm both. He's as big as I am. I don't know how to fight with a mouse and I haven't got a weapon to use against him."

"Well, you better think of something Jake! The clock is ticking and time is running out."

"I know that Max, and I'm trying to find something that I can use to fight with."

In desperation Jake looked around for some item—any sort of object—that he could use as a weapon. But there didn't seem to be anything available—everything was bolted down, wired into the circuitry, or fastened securely to the surrounding frame. He continued to look about, searching for anything that he could use to attack the formidable, gray rodent-obstacle that was blocking his objective. Just when the specter of defeat was closing in on him, he saw five ceramic fuses in a clip holder attached to the frame.

These were spare fuses to be used as replacements for any blown fuses in the circuitry. Jake thought that he might possibly use them. Anyway, it was worth a try because there didn't seem to be anything else nearby. Using both hands, he pulled a fuse from the clip. The fuse was heavy but he managed to raise the it above his head and throw it at the mouse. The flying projectile struck the rodent's flank. The mouse was stunned by the impact—perhaps confused by the sudden, unexpected blow that apparently came from nowhere—it flinched but remained in place.

Jake pulled another fuse from the clip and hurled it at the mouse. This time the fuse hit the rodent in the head. At this point the mouse decided that it had endured enough punishment and it ran for cover and disappeared deep into the surrounding maze of computer circuitry. With the mouse gone, Jake could approach the transmitter modules and attach transmitter bugs to the nodes. In a few minutes, he had the transmitter bugs in place. Now, all he had to do was retrace his path and scram back to the Winnebago.

Jake turned and stepped gingerly across the horizonal circuit board to reach the back panel. He climbed down the perforated grid to the service panel then crawled through the vent port. He breathed a sigh of relief because it seemed that the hardest part of his job was behind him. He walked out of the computer room assuming that the rest would go smooth and easy, but there was another danger, a potential threat, still in his path.

Jake stepped into the hall and that's when he saw it. The big orange cat was still in the hallway. It hadn't moved and was still sleeping in the hallway. During the tangle in the computer circuitry with the big, gray mouse, he had forgotten all about the slumbering beast. He stood in place, motionless, as studied the inert animal. From all appearances it looked like the creature was dead to the world, enveloped in a heavy stupor, insensitive to its surroundings.

Jake knew that he would have to get past the beast before he could return to safety. He had inched by the dormant cat before, so maybe he could do it again. He started to tip-toe down the hall, being careful to hug the wall opposite to the sleeping cat. As he advanced, Jake kept his eyes glued to the figure of the motionless feline. He continued to move closer and closer to the animal—all the time remaining wary and alert to any hint of movement from the creature, but the feline remained still and quiet, unaware that a miniature human being was trying to slip by.

Soon Jake was directly across from the cat, and it seemed like he was going to get safely by the feline without awakening it. But then something unexpected and unlucky happened; one of the suction handles in his backpack had been jostled during Jake's recent mouse-fight and was now precariously close to the opening of the pack. Jake had carelessly neglected to zip the pack fully closed after he extracted the transmitter bugs and that oversight would now have serious consequences.

Just as Jake was crossing in front of the cat, the suction handle fell from his pack and hit the floor. It made a noise—not a loud noise—but just enough to wake the beast. Jake turned and bent over to retrieve the handle and at the same time he looked over his shoulder to see if there was any reaction from the cat. He saw the animal's eyes open to a narrow slit, and when the cat saw Jake it became alert and its eyes opened wide. At that moment Jake knew that he was in deep trouble.

CHAPTER 13

There was no time to lose. No time for vacillation or uncertainty. Jake knew that the feline beast was coming to life and about to pounce on him; he had to get away as fast as possible. He sprinted away from the waking feline menace and made a mad dash down the hall. The cat, now fully awake and alert, sprang up and tried to go after the fleeing human prey. The beast set its legs in motion but its feet did not immediately gain traction on the slippery floor and for a brief second the feline was running in place—with its legs pedaling frantically—but not going anywhere. Suddenly its padded paws caught onto the surface of the floor and the animal took off like a shot in hot pursuit of Jake.

Now Jake knew that he could never hope to outrun the oncoming beast. His only chance for survival was to find someplace where he could escape from the deadly fangs and sharp claws of the ferocious tiger that was closing in on him. Then he saw a room ahead—the door was open. Maybe he could find some niche, some nook or cranny in that room that would shelter him from the clutches of the monster cat that was right behind him.

He burst into the room and immediately saw a desk against the far wall. The cat was almost on him—there wasn't a moment to hesitate. Just as the cat was ready to pounce, Jake took a flying leap, landed on his stomach and slid across the polished floor into the shallow space under the desk. He glided on the slick floor to the safety of the back wall and was able to avoid the cat's grasp by a hairsbreadth. The cat stopped at the desk, crouched down and looked under the desk for its elusive prey. The animal was too big to crawl in the shallow space between the bottom of the desk and the floor and its paw wasn't long enough to get a good swipe at Jake who was out of reach against the back wall.

However, the feline predator was not about to abandon the quarry. It lay flattened against the floor with its tail wagging, and waited eagerly, watching with wide-eyed anticipation for its prey, Jake the human rodent, to come out into the opening. Now it was a stalemate with man and beast eyeing each other to see which would give up first.

Jake was trapped and he was painfully aware that time was running out for him. He had expended a lot of energy and had accelerated his metabolism. That meant that soon—very soon—the atoms in his body would be energized and expand. He would soon start to grow to his full size. When that happened, it would be easy for him to chase the cat away but then he would be trapped inside a bigger enclosure, the building complex of *Dense Fog.*

He would be locked within the walls of the enemy fortress with no escape, no place to hide, and no way to avoid detection. Then he would face an even greater menace than the house cat. He would be at the mercy of the security guards who monitored the premises for intruders and external threats. When they discovered him, the mission would be compromised and he would be eliminated.

Jake was aware that the body metamorphosis might kick in at any moment and he knew that he had to act fast because his options were few. His immediate priority was to get away from the stalking cat. He pulled the suction handles from his backpack and used them to climb up the back wall behind the desk. He reached the desk top and crawled over to the front edge where he peered down at the cat crouching on the floor below. The beast was still intently looking under the desk trying discover where its prey had suddenly disappeared to. The cat obviously had no idea that Jake was now on top of the desk observing the action from above.

This could be the break that Jake was hoping for, and he hatched a bold plan. The cat was vulnerable to an attack from above and if he could find something—a heavy object like a paper weight—then he could drop it on the cat's head, knock the beast out of commission and make his getaway. He looked around the desk for something that he could use as an aerial bomb.

As he was looking about for something heavy enough to drop on the unsuspecting critter, Max's voice came over the communicator, "Jake, Jake, what's happening? According to our monitor screen you are in some office near the computer room. Is that right? What are you doing there? You should be making your way out of the building."

"Max," replied Jake with impatience, "I can't talk now! I'm trying to fight off a cat that thinks I'm a mouse."

"A cat?! You're playing with a cat! Jake you've got to get out of there. You don't have time to fool with a cat. You've got to get a move on."

"Damn it, Max! I know that. I'm trying to…Oh never mind!"

This was no time for long-winded explanations. Jake switched off his communicator and resumed his quest for an aerial bomb when he began to feel some stirrings within his body. He felt internal vibrations, subtle at first then growing in intensity, and he knew that the transformation process was starting in his body.

There was nothing Jake could do to forestall the process so he sat down on the desktop and let the change happen. A weird tingling sensation began to course through his body. This was followed by peculiar feelings that seemed like a combination of orgasm, massage, and electrical shock therapy and he instinctively knew that the atomic particles, the protons and electrons in his body were moving apart, diverging to their natural positions. He was growing. He looked at his hands and feet. They were getting bigger and he was aware that his whole body was stretching and widening. This came at an inopportune moment but there was nothing he could do but sit still and let the process continue and at the same time hope that he would not grow to full size.

These strange body vibrations lasted for a long minute, and then they stopped. He had grown, but mercifully not to full size. This was just the first stage of the growth process. There would be others but with luck they would come later when he was safely outside the confines of the *Dense Fog* Fortress—that is if he could escape to the outside.

He looked at his limbs and torso and tried to gauge how big he had become. He couldn't be sure of his new size because he couldn't see his whole self; but by examining his limbs, he estimated that he doubled in size and was now about twelve- to fourteen-inches tall. Jake decided that he was big enough to go on the offensive and take on the unsuspecting cat.

He crawled to the edge of the desk and peered down. The cat was still in a crouch with its tail swishing from side to side and its eyes fixated on the area under the desk; it was still searching for the mouse-man that had escaped its clutches and waiting in anticipation of its reappearance. Jake stood up, took a deep breath, then jumped from the edge of the desktop. He kept his legs wide apart and he landed on the cat's back with a leg against either side of the critter. He grabbed handfuls of the beast's fur and pressed his knees against the animal's flanks.

The cat was taken completely by surprise. It didn't know where this sudden weight on its back had come from; but it acted instinctively by rising up and arching its spine in an attempt to buck the unwanted rider off its back. The cat jumped up and down in a variety of contortions and maneuvers in an effort to dislodge the rider, but Jake held on tenaciously to the animal's fur and clamped his legs against its sides. For a few moments it looked like a scene from a miniature rodeo competition with a cowboy riding on a bucking bronco. Finally, the beast rolled over and Jake had to release his grip and push away so he wouldn't be crushed by the weight of the rolling feline body.

Jake scrambled to his feet and backed against the nearest wall. Man and beast were now face to face, and the angry cat attacked with a vengeance. It swiped at Jake with its paw but the sharp claws only glanced off the bomb-cloth fabric of Jake's body suit. Undaunted, the cat opened its mouth, bared its fangs and moved in for a kill. When the animal came within range, Jake pushed his left hand against the beast's nose then shot a straight right punch to the face. The cat recoiled a little and Jake swung a left hook to the nose followed by two more straight rights.

This barrage of punches had their effect. The cat raised up on its hind legs and rubbed its nose with its front paws. Jake saw this backaway action as a chance to escape from the onslaught of the beast. He dove onto the floor, slid on his stomach between the cat's rear legs and came out behind the animal. When the cat dropped its paws and looked around for Jake, he was nowhere in sight.

While the cat searched in bewilderment for its missing prey, Jake stood up, seized its long furry tail and he pulled hard. This sudden move pulled the back legs out from under the feline adversary and it fell flat on its stomach with its legs splayed out in four directions. The cat was dazed and completely off-balance. Jake continued pulling on the furry tail while he turned around in a circle. As Jake spun around the helpless animal was pulled in a wide arc around the slippery floor. Jake made three complete rotations then he released the tail and the cat sailed across the floor like a spinning hockey puck and crashed into a wastepaper basket.

The cat was dazed and confused but it was still conscious. Jake knew that in a few seconds the ferocious tiger-cat would shake off the effects of the spinning crash, and regain its senses. He had to get away while he had the chance. Jake ran out of the office and darted down the hall. He had a head start but he knew that the angry cat would be in hot pursuit as soon as it recovered its equilibrium. That wasn't long in coming.

The cat rose to its full height and shook its head. It didn't quite know what had happened, but propelled by its predatory instincts and energized by the animal urge to capture and kill, the beast took up the chase and went after the fleeing Jake.

As he was running down the hall at top speed, Jake knew that he had to find a way to break off his adversary's attack and chase it away so that he could get out of the building. *But how to do that?* There didn't seem to be anything available—nothing that he could use as a weapon and no place to hide. When he reached the end of the hall and turned the corner he saw something that could be the expedient that he was looking for.

About a quarter of the way down the hall was a slop sink. Situated on the floor before the sink was mop in a bucket. Jake ran to the bucket, jumped up on the rim and reached over to the mop; he grabbed the handle and shimmied up the shaft to the edge of the slop sink. He jumped from the edge of the sink to the faucet and sat on the connecting water pipe. He looked down the spigot and saw a short, black hose screwed to the spout. Jake reached for the hose, grabbed the nozzle then braced himself against the faucet body and he waited for the oncoming cat.

By now the attacking cat had turned the corner, run down the hall and had reached the slop sink. The sharp eyes of the rapacious feline looked up and saw Jake sitting smugly on the faucet above and with single-minded purpose, the cat jumped to the edge of the sink. For a moment, but adversaries remained motionless, as if in a state of suspended animation, as if each was waiting to see what the other would do.

Just as the cat was ready to pounce, Jake aimed the hose and kicked the faucet open. A burst of water shot out from the hose and splashed the cat in the face. *That did it!* The furry beast had enough. The cat dropped from the sink to the floor and ran away down the hall with its tail held straight up like a flag pole.

Jake watched the critter run away and shouted after it, "Serves you right, you filthy beast! You needed a bath anyway."

Now the cat was gone and a major problem had been eliminated, but Jake still had to make his getaway. He knew that he had grown too big to crawl out through the HVAC ducts. He had to find another way out. As he looked around, searching for some means of escape, he saw a window across the hall. It was a small window—about half the size of a normal, double hung-window—and it was high up—about six feet from the floor, but it was half open.

Jake reasoned that if he could get up to the window sill then he could crawl through the open window to the outside. *How to get from the floor to the window sill?* He could use his suction handles to climb up the wall but then he had a sudden inspiration—there was something else that he could use to get up to the window—something that would be easier and faster. There was the bucket and mop by the slop sink.

Jake dropped down from the sink. The bucket was on wheels and he was able to push it—with the mop inside—across the hall to the small window. When the two pieces were in position he pushed the mop handle against the wall and climbed the haft to the half-open window. There was just enough space between the sill and sash for him to squeeze through the window and emerge to the outside.

He stood outside on the window ledge and looked down. The guard dogs had already sensed his presence and had congregated, looking up and eyeing him from below. Jake realized that any slip on his part would drop him down to the ground where the savage mongrels were waiting for the chance to tear him to pieces.

But he could avoid that grim fate if he could climb up to the roof. There he would be away from the dogs and he could call for the drone to pick him up and fly beyond the confines of *Dense Fog*. Then he would be home free. Escape was almost within his grasp—*or so he thought.*

CHAPTER 14

As Jake stood on the window ledge looking down at the anxious, salivating canines that were monitoring his every move, he was painfully aware that his metabolic clock was ticking and soon the atoms in his would body burst out to assume their natural configuration and return him to his full-grown self. He wanted to be far away from *Dense Fog* before that happened.

Somehow, he had to get to the roof. He looked about and saw that to his left—less than six feet away—was a drain pipe that ran from ground level to the top of the building. From his vantage point, the pipe looked climbable, but first he had to get to it. Fortunately, there was a narrow perimeter shoulder that ran from the window ledge to the drain pipe and it was just wide enough for Jake to traverse.

He pressed his body against the wall and sidestepped away from the window toward the drain pipe. Jake slowly and gingerly maneuvered along the shoulder by extending his leg then bringing the other against it, slowly by repeating this maneuver he was able to advance in increments toward the drain pipe. At the same time, he was ever-conscious that one careless slip would cause him to fall to the carnivorous jaws of the vicious mutts waiting below.

After a few tense moments, he reached the pipe and he felt an emotional release. But he still had to get up to the roof. He examined the pipe and masonry wall pondering how he was going to make the climb. He couldn't use the suction handles on either masonry wall or the drainpipe because one was too porous the other too curved. But he found that if he wedged himself between the pipe and wall, he could push his fingers and toes in the joints in the masonry wall and climb brick by brick. Up he went. It was tedious going and it required all his strength but at last he reached the roof and he let out an enormous sigh of relief.

He took a minute to rest and collect his thoughts then he tapped the communicator button on his cheek pad.

"Max, it's me Jake. Can you hear me? I'm on the roof and I need you to send the drone so I can get the hell away from here."

"Yeah Jake! I can hear you. It's good to hear your voice again. You okay? Last time we talked you said that you were fighting with a cat. How did you get away from it?"

"My metabolism kicked in and I grew a few inches taller so I was able to push the beast off. Never mind that now, I've got to get off this roof pronto. Just send the drone."

"Gladly Jake! I'll get Spike to launch it right away. It will be there in…oh wait a minute…"

"What? Why wait a minute? Max, time is running out, I'm going to grow soon. We can't wait a minute. Send the drone now!"

"Well Jake, I'm not sure we can do that. There may be a problem."

"Max, what are you talking about? What kind of problem?"

"Jake, you said that you were able to fight the cat off because you grew in size. You're bigger now. How big are you?"

"I donno know. Maybe about twelve inches tall. Possibly fourteen inches. I really can't be sure. Why? What's the problem?"

"Well Jake, remember I told you that the load capacity of the drone is only five pounds. If you've grown bigger then you may be too big and too heavy for it."

Jake thought about what Max had just said and he realized that Max was right; at his present size he would most likely be too big for the small drone.

"Okay Max, you're probably right. So, scratch the drone. What's the backup plan?"

Max didn't answer immediately, instead there was a lapse of silence—a long pause.

"Max," said Jake impatiently, "time is running out. What's the backup? What is plan B?"

"Well Jake," replied Max tentatively, "you see it's like this—"

Suddenly Jake realized why Max had been so silent and so hesitant all of a sudden.

"Damn it, Max! You don't have a backup plan, do you? You haven't thought beyond this moment."

"Now Jake, don't overreact. It is true that we don't have a backup plan, but you have to understand that *Strategic Planning* did not anticipate that you would have a fight with a mouse and a cat, so naturally they couldn't foresee you getting so big so soon. They didn't foresee you getting too heavy for the drone. After all Jake, you have to keep in mind that we're all human and cannot predict the future so, naturally we can't plan for every contingency. You have to remain realistic and maintain your sense of proportions."

"That's easy for you to say. You're not the one stuck on this roof. You're not the one who is going to grow to full size at any minute. When that happens, I'll be trapped up here. How are you going to get me off this roof?"

"Now Jake," said Max, attempting to adopt a soothing, pacifying demeanor, "calm down. I can tell by the sound of your voice that you're starting to get agitated and it's not good for you to get excited. That will only raise your metabolic rate and cause you to grow faster. It might even distort your perspective and make you lose your ability to think rationally. You must remain calm in this situation."

"Max, you rat bastard—"

"Oh Jake! I'm surprised at you using such coarse language. There's no need to resort to profanity. And berating me with your vituperation! That offends me, Jake. It really does. You have to remember that I have feelings too, and I'm sensitive to abusive invective. I don't deserve—"

"Oh, stop sounding like you just ate a dictionary. You're fretting about your bruised feelings while I'm about to get trapped up here and see the rest of my life go down the toilet. What are you going to do to get me off this roof?"

"Jake, I told you that we're working on it. Peter, Spike and myself are going to sit down and see if we can come up with a workable plan. In the meantime, you must try and figure out some solution from your end. After all, it's not fair to expect us to solve all your problems. You must take some of the responsibility too, and try—"

"Oh, shut the hell up and thanks for nothing!" With that, Jake tapped his transmitter button and silenced Max Beltrane's patronizing voice.

Jake looked around. He realized that he would get no help from the team in the Winnebago and that it was entirely up to him to find a way to escape from the roof and from entrapment in *Dense Fog*. His rescue would depend totally on his imagination and his ingenuity.

In desperation, Jake walked around looking, searching, for some possible way to get off the roof. At first, the situation seemed hopeless, but then he saw something that just might work. He saw a vertical pole near the edge of the roof. A power line ran from the pole over the dog pit to a light pole beyond the fence. The power line was supported by a braided steel cable.

As Jake studied the installation, a daring plan started to formulate in his mind. He imagined that if he draped a strap over the cable, and gripped both ends, he could slide down the line, pass over the predatory guard dogs to the light pole on the other side of the perimeter fence.

Yes, he thought to himself, *it just might work*. Actually, it had to work, because he was painfully aware that in his present circumstances, he didn't have any other options.

Jake removed the waist strap from his backpack and clenched it in his teeth. Then he climbed up the vertical pole to the steel cable above. When he reached the top, he took the strap from his teeth with his left hand and flipped one end over the line. He grabbed that end with his right hand. Now he was holding the strap with both hands and his legs were still wrapped around the pole. All his had to do was kick free of the pole and hopefully he would slide down the cable to light pole on the other side of the fence. That was the intention, the plan, the scheme, but *would it work?* He was about to find out.

He dropped his legs and pushed away from the vertical pole and immediately he started to slide down the steel cable away from the roof. He was dangling from the cable, hanging with both hands onto the strap that was looped over the braided, steel support cable. He was making smooth, steady progress sliding away from the roof toward the light pole on the other side of the perimeter fence. The voracious pack of dogs was below, looking up, following his progress. Jake knew that he was in a precarious position, but he felt that as long as he had the strength to hang on, and as long as the strap did not break, then he could make it to safety.

It seemed that all was going smoothly, but then he hit an obstacle. It was a ceramic insulator in the cable. When his looped strap hit the insulator, he stopped sliding. He was halted at the worst possible place, halfway between the roof and the fence, suspended directly over the yard where the pack of ferocious canines was watching and waiting below. He had to get past this obstacle or all would be lost. He tried swinging his legs in wide circles in an effort to rise up and bypass the insulator.

Eventually after executing a variety of gyrations and aerial maneuvers, he succeeded in levitating over and beyond the hang-up. After that, he glided effortlessly to the light pole. He wrapped his legs and arms around the pole and slid down to land on the solid ground. It was a good feeling to know that he was on *terra firma* and safe and sound beyond the clutches of the enemy, but he was exhausted beyond belief. He needed a place to sit down, rest, and recover his strength. Jake walked over to a nearby tree and sat down on the ground. He sat there with his hands on his lap, his feet stretched out before him, his back against the tree trunk and his mind a blank slate.

Then a surprising thing happened—a small, cotton-tail rabbit suddenly and unexpectedly appeared from out of the bush and hopped up and sat beside Jake's outstretched leg. The bunny found a morsel of vegetation and started munching on it, while at the same time, it seemed totally oblivious to Jake's presence.

Jake sat there, motionless, just watching the rabbit nibble on the green sprouts that it had picked up, and he was pleased to be so close to this innocent little creature. He thought to himself that it was as if he was part of this little rabbit's world—that his diminutive size had allowed him to enter and participate in a world that up till this moment had been completely unknown to him. At this moment he was as if he was an active member of the small animal kingdom and not merely an observer.

In reflection, he realized that in the last hour, he had struggled with a giant cockroach, chased a mouse and battled with a house cat. He had confronted these creatures on their turf and on their terms as one of them. Jake watched the little rabbit, absorbed with munching on the green sprigs before it, and he had the impulse to try and make friends with this innocent, furry creature. He wanted to share the moment with the furry bunny because he felt that his miniature stature gave him a common bond with this woodland rabbit.

Just as Jake was about to stretch his hand out to pet the animal, he felt internal stirrings and vibrations rising in his body and he knew that the final stage of his body's metamorphosis was beginning. The atoms within him were starting to push apart to regain their natural dimensions and soon he would be returned to his normal size. Jake sat there, passive and calm, allowing the change to play out. He could feel his body and limbs getting larger and longer. At the same time. he continued to watch the little bunny wondering if the critter would notice the transformation happening next to it, but it seemed that the rabbit was completely focused on nibbling the greenery and remained unconscious to the fact that the human being next to it was turning into a giant.

In a matter of minutes, the transfiguration was complete; Jake was fully restored to his normal size. Now he followed his impulse to reach out and pet the cute and innocent little bunny peacefully chewing the verdant sprigs. When the animal felt Jake's large hand touch its back it turned and looked in surprise and horror at the big leviathan that had suddenly, unexpectedly appeared beside it. The frightened little creature sprang away and bounded off disappearing into the surrounding bushes.

Jake looked after the fleeing rabbit and said, "I'm sorry Mr. Rabbit. I just wanted to be friends, but I guess that's not possible because I'm now a big human monster and no longer part of your world. Well, so be it!"

It was now time to return to the real world of espionage. Jake tapped his communicator button and spoke into the mike, "Max, it's me, Jake. Can you hear me?"

"Yes Jake, I hear you loud and clear. I tell you that it is wonderful to hear your voice again. At this moment I'm looking at the monitor and it appears that you're off the roof and outside the compound. Is that right? Are you free and clear of *Dense Fog*?"

"Yeah Max, I managed to find a way to get off the roof and land beyond the perimeter fence. Now, what I need you to do—"

Max interrupted, "Oh Jake! That's wonderful. You were able to rescue yourself without anyone helping you. You focused on the problem, applied yourself to find a solution and utilized your own resources. Isn't that a wonderful feeling, knowing that when the chips are down, and the future looks dark, you have the aptitude, versatility, and self-skills to cross the finish line by yourself? That should give you a glow of self-satisfaction knowing that you can come through, overcome the obstacles and score a touchdown when you want to. That's what I call the winning attitude and it's what separates the champion from the average player."

Jake sat against the tree, listening, saying nothing, just letting Max voice his sophomoric soliloquy about the virtues and rewards of self-reliance, determination and autonomy. It was a tedious monologue and he wanted to tell Max to shut up but he simply didn't have the energy to protest. So, he let Max drone on, hoping that the end of his prolix would come sometime in the near future.

Eventually Max did pause and Jake used the opportunity to speak up. "Yeah, yeah Max, I'm overjoyed that I have outstanding talent and marvelous abilities, but can you stifle your enthusiasm long enough to come and pick me up so that we can get out of here."

"Of course, Jake, I was coming to that. I'll tell Peter to get in the driver's seat and we'll come around and pick you up. Where exactly are you?"

"I'm in the bushes and trees off the side of the road about ten feet from the entrance gate of this place."

There was a long pause. To Jake it seemed like an ominous silence. Finally, Max spoke up.

"You say that you're about ten feet from the entrance gate?"

"Yeah," replied Jake. "That's right."

"Well, then we can't drive over to pick you up."

"Why the hell not?" asked an angry Jake.

"Come on Jake. Use your head. The security forces inside the building are probably monitoring the fence and gate for suspicious activity. If they see a big Winnebago drive up to the gate and then see somebody come out of the woods and climb into the vehicle, they are gonna wonder what gives and will start to investigate. They might stumble onto our operation and then everything that we worked for will go up in smoke.

"No Jake, it's better if we sit tight and you come to us. We're only about five miles away. You should be able to walk that distance in no time."

"Five miles! Ah come on Max—"

"Now Jake, don't be a whiner. Five miles is nothing to a guy like you who is in top physical condition. Well, it's getting late and we have a long drive back to the city, so you'd best get a move on. We'll be waiting for you.

"Oh, one more thing; don't go onto the road just yet, or you may be spotted. There's a bend in the road about a mile up from the front gate. Stay undercover in the bush until you pass that bend, then you'll be out of sight and you can cross over to the road. I can't wait to see you and hear about your adventure in *Dense Fog*."

The dialog ended on that note. Jake remained sitting against the tree trying to summon the energy to rise up and set out on the five-mile hike that he would have to endure to get back to the Winnebago.

It was a prospect that he didn't relish but he knew that there was no way around it. Finally, after a few more minutes of rest, he pushed against the tree trunk and rose to a standing position. As he stood up, it seemed that every muscle, fiber, and joint in his body telegraphed some ache or pain. He felt like he had been run over by a garbage truck.

Jake started walking, and respecting Max's cautionary exhortation, he stayed off the road, taking advantage of the cover that the woods provided. Walking at night in the brush would be difficult because the vegetation was dense, the pathway was dark and opaque, and visibility was limited. In addition, there were rocks, vines, puddles, and holes to step over or walk around. As Jake trekked through the bush, frequently tripped and stumbled and every time that he lost his footing, he cursed Max Beltrane.

After hiking, stumbling, and cursing for almost an hour, Jake reached the bend in the road and he exited the woods to venture onto the pavement. Walking on the road was easier than going through the woods and Jake was able to make good time on the last leg of his hike. Nevertheless, he was tired and as he walked along the road, he wondered if he would have the strength to continue. Just when he felt that he was about to consume the final dregs of his endurance, he saw the Winnebago.

He walked up to the side of the vehicle, pounded on the door and said, "Max, it's me Jake! Open up and let me in."

Immediately the side door flew open revealing the figure of Max Beltrane standing in the door frame.

"Oh Jake!" he said with over-the-top enthusiasm. "It is so good to see you. Come inside, sit down and take load off. You must be tired after your long walk."

"That's putting it mildly," said Jake sarcastically as he stepped into the interior of the Winnebago and plopped down in the nearest seat. Peter and Spike were sitting nearby and gave Jake nods and closed-mouthed smiles of approval on his return.

"Well," said Max, "how about a nice cold drink to wet your whistle. Would you like that?"

"Yeah, that sounds good. Have you got a cold beer?"

"Jake! I'm surprised at you. I remind you that we are on company time, executing an important mission. Surely, you must be aware that alcoholic beverages are counterproductive to the strict discipline required for an operation of this magnitude. I should think that you—"

"All right already Max! Skip the lesson in boy scout ethics. What have you got to drink?"

"How about a nice cold Coke?"

Jake nodded approval and Max went to the cooler. He took a handful of ice cubes and dumped them into a plastic tumbler. Then he pulled out a can of Coca Cola. He pulled up the tab to open the can and poured the effervescent liquid into the tumbler. He handed it to Jake.

Jake took the beverage, raised it to his mouth and took a big gulp. He savored the effects of the cool soda as it flowed past his mouth and down his parched throat. It was a good, refreshing feeling and it gave him a sensation of well-being. He leaned back against the seat rest and was starting to relax when Max spoke up again.

"Well men," he said in a posture of inflated self-importance, "I think that we can all congratulate ourselves on a job well-done. Yes indeed! I don't mind telling you that this was a difficult mission, but we all pulled together and came through with flying colors. And I must say that I am proud to know that I provided you with the leadership and guidance that motivated you to perform your tasks so efficiently."

Jake listened to Max's pompous palaver with growing annoyance. Finally, he said, "Max what the hell are you talking about? What did you do? I'm the one who got shrunk to mouse-size. I'm the one who crawled through the vent shafts to find the computer and insert the transmitter bugs. I'm the one who fought with the animal life in the building and I'm the one who had to walk five miles to get back here. I did all of that while you sat back here on your butt and did nothing."

Peter and Spike listened to Jake's angry rebuke and said nothing but they both smiled and nodded in recognition of the truth of Jake's words. Max, however, was not to be silenced. He assumed a demeanor of distress and anguish.

He said, "Oh Jake, I am surprised at you, and disappointed. Yes, disappointed. I simply cannot believe that you want to hog all the glory, eminence and importance for yourself. Your attitude really smacks of hubris and condescension. I would have thought that you were incapable of such base emotions.

"It is true that I did not go through the reducing machine and I did not go into the *Dense Fog* building with you. At least not in body, but I was with you in spirit. I was here in the control station monitoring your every move, ready to guide you and assist you at every turn and I believe I deserve a lot of credit for that."

Jake said nothing. He just sat there, quietly sipping his soda as he listened to Max ramble on with his bombastic discourse. And all the time that Max was talking, Jake glared at him and silently wondered to himself how many years in prison he would get if he strangled Max Beltrane.

The End